A ONE-WAY TICKET TO RUIN

DANIEL GRABOWSKI

Thankyou again, Marie, I'm told this one is even better than the first - I hope you'll agree!

D.

DS PRODUCTIONS

Copyright © 2023 by Daniel Grabowski

Published by DS Productions

All rights reserved.

This book may not be duplicated in any way without the express written consent of the publisher, except in the form of brief excerpts or quotations for the purposes of review.

The information contained herein is for the personal use of the reader and may not be incorporated in any commercial programs or other books, databases, or any kind of software without written consent of the publisher or author. Making copies of this book or any portion of it, for any purpose is a violation of United States copyright laws.

This is a work of fiction. Names, characters, places, and incidents either are the product of the author's imagination or are used fictitiously. Any resemblance to actual persons, living or dead, events, or locales is entirely coincidental.

ISBN: 9798378704101

❦ Created with Vellum

PROLOGUE

Kyle Barnes was in pain. Lots of pain. He couldn't see anything, but he could feel the scratching fibers of the sack over his head. He could feel the blood oozing from the split in his ballooned lip. He could feel the ropes biting into his wrists and ankles; he felt a buzzing in his fingers and toes. He could hear the whining creak of the chair with every shift he made, desperate to find some semblance of comfort. But none was to be found. With every slap, punch, and kick, he'd felt the chair groan along with him.

"Come on, Kyle, you know what you need to do," said a male voice, soft and low, with a friendly quality. He did most of the talking. Kyle thought he maybe quite liked the sound of himself too on account of how much he went on. "Just tell me what I need to know, my friend. And this will stop. My associate will stop putting you through this wholly unnecessary ordeal and you can walk right on out of here and on your merry way."

Kyle coughed.

"Or we carry on."

"I . . . I told you already . . ." Kyle began before pausing because of the burning in his lungs and the stinging in his lip. He screwed his eyelids together and continued, "It's gonna be on a train out of Rathdrum."

"Mateo."

A fist struck Kyle's left cheek. His head buzzed with fresh anguish. Mateo only spoke with his fists. Kyle grumbled through the pain, and he felt the blood drip from his mouth, soaking into the sack.

Kyle knew there were others in the room. He could hear their movements: their shuffles and their steps. But they did not speak. He wondered if the two men who had grabbed him were in here. Maybe one of them was Mateo, currently working Kyle over with his fists.

"We know *that*, Kyle. Come on now, we've been through this. I don't need to know the where or the how. We got that already!" Kyle could hear the thudding of his bootsteps as he paced the room. "What I need to know, right now, and when I do *all* of your suffering will end, is *when*." The boots stopped their thumping.

A loaded silence hung in the air.

Kyle had two choices. The first was to keep quiet and most definitely die. Alternatively, Kyle could hand this man and his friend with the mean fists what they wanted, and they *might* let him go home to his wife and his little baby girl Allie. Oh, how he missed her little butter-colored curls and her plump cheeks. He'd no longer be an agent of the Pinkertons, but he would still have his life. By his own count, he had already lost at least two teeth and had several ribs that were at the very least severely bruised.

That was enough to lose.

"T-two o'clock," Kyle sputtered. "It's gonna be on the two o'clock to Spokane."

"Really?" Mr. Friendly said. "Now, you wouldn't be spinning me and my friends here a yarn, would you, Kyle? That would be awful rude."

"N-no," Kyle said and did his best to shake his head but stopped at the searing pain that shot through his jaw when he did. "Please, sir. That's all I know. I'd just like to go home to my family and my daughter. Spokane. Two o'clock. On my family's life, I swear it."

"And Mr. Osborne's safe will be onboard that train, yes?"

"Yes, sir."

Kyle heard hands clap together.

"Fantastic! See now, Kyle, was that so hard? All of that pain and suffering could have been avoided. And we are almost done here. Then you can go on your merry way, back to your family and your sweet little daughter. I'm sure they'll be *real* happy to see you."

"A-almost done?" Kyle felt the faltering in his voice.

"Sure. I just need to know the security details. Obviously minus yourself, just what measures has the wonderful Pinkerton Agency taken to protect Ellis Osborne's safe?"

"Well," Kyle began and then coughed up phlegm and blood. It felt like something was loose in his lungs. He gathered himself and then continued, "The safe is in a private compartment in the rear . . . the luggage store." Kyle had to pause because of the fire in his jaw.

"Kyle?" Mr. Friendly sounded impatient.

"That'll . . . that'll be locked up with a man inside. Allen his name is. Allen Avery. Then in another car, there'll be Phelps." Kyle hacked up a glob of red. "Old . . . but he's good."

Another loaded silence.

"Is that it? Nobody else?"

"Not on the train. It's a pretty tough safe."

"We're a pretty tough crew. And safes are our specialty. Ain't that right, Leon?"

"Yup," came a voice that was more of a grunt.

"Leon's real good with safes. And blowin' stuff up. He's a maestro. Just like Mateo here is with his fists."

Another slam into Kyle's cheek. He howled. Another tooth had loosened.

"*God damn it,* Mateo! What the hell are you doin'? That's not an invitation to hit the man. *Christ!*"

"*Lo siento.*" A husky whisper.

"Okay, everybody, listen up." Mr. Friendly's voice had raised and taken on a more authoritative quality. "We've got what we needed. Tomorrow, we head to the station, and we execute the plan. We get on independently, separate cars, too. We wait until we're a few miles out.

Brett, you take out the driver, ready to stop the train once we've taken care of the passengers. Mateo, you're in charge of switching the tracks. Then you and Brett keep an eye on the cars while Leon and I deal with the safe. Knowles . . ." That was a name Kyle hadn't heard before. Five of them in total. He'd bring this to the attention of the Pinkerton Agency the moment he could. "You're on standby. Blend in, and if you can, identify that other Pinkerton so we can make sure the *sumbitch* ain't no problem. We all clear?"

Voices in agreement rolled all around him.

"All right," Mr. Friendly said, punctuating it with a clap of his hands. "Well then, let's have a drink and get a good night's sleep."

"Uh, Eddie? Boss?"

Eddie. So *that* was his name.

"Yes, Brett?"

"What about *him*?"

"Oh, shoot. . . yes! Kyle!" Eddie said and sucked in air through his teeth. Kyle felt a twinge of dread. He wasn't so sure he liked the sudden new tone in Eddie's voice. "I forgot you were there for a second. Guess we'd better let you go now and have you on your way. You won't go squealin' like a little stuck piglet now, will ya?"

"No. Absolutely not," Kyle said, shaking his head through the pain. They were actually going to let him go! He was going to see his baby girl and her butter-colored curls again. He felt stinging in the corners of his eyes.

"Mateo, would you?"

Kyle didn't hear the man walk over. Nor did he feel the loosening of his restraints. Instead, he heard the shift of something across leather. Then a metallic click. It sounded familiar, like the thumbing back of a hammer on a revolver.

1

A TRAIN TO SPOKANE

Since Jesse Clayton had told Winona that he just might stay, they'd watched two sunsets together. They'd spent their time up at her father's ranch, keeping mostly to her room. Unfortunately, they couldn't be as voracious as they'd hoped, given Winona's shoulder and Jesse's ribs. Still, pain and all, they'd managed to make a mighty time of it. But like all good things, it eventually came to an end.

Wilkerson had been convinced to stay, too. Not by Jesse, in spite of his best efforts, but by the tab still open to him at the Jewel.

Having traveled a few hours, the party of three was approaching the town of Rathdrum. Formerly known as Westwood, Rathdrum had in recent times undergone a bit of identity crisis, Wilkerson had explained, and was thus renamed after the hometown of an Irish pioneer.

What struck Jesse was its size. Rathdrum was Fortune many times over. Structures spread out from the creek, and the spire of the church stood sentinel in the middle of it all. It looked down upon all of them, a reminder that God was always watching.

The wagon rode down Main Street, and Jesse could see all manner of stores along it. Passing the barber's made Jesse think he was due a shave. Main Street itself was abuzz with traffic. Wagons inched up and down, as dozens of people strolled across the roads, dipping between wagons and slogging through the thick, soupy mud. Jesse had spotted half a dozen saloons and at least three hotels before Wilkerson finally pulled his wagon to a halt.

"End of the line, you two!" Wilkerson said. "You hop off here; I must find somewhere to set down."

Jesse hopped off first. When he splashed into the mud, he noted the bullet holes in the wagon, and his mind wandered briefly back to the night that Christie had died. He felt the guilt fleetingly, before pushing it out and looking back up at Winona. She brought out a smile from him. He offered his hand, and she took it, then he helped her down from the wagon into the mud. She hiked her dress up above the ankles slightly, to keep it untarnished.

"Thank you, Tobias," Jesse said.

"You're welcome and enjoy your train ride. I hear they are quite the experience!"

"Speak for yourself," Winona said. "I've heard they're big and loud. I'm all a shiver just thinkin' about it."

"You know," Wilkerson started as he plopped into the mud. "I might have something to help with that, Miss Squires." He opened one of the small compartments of his wagon and rummaged around. He plucked out a small glass bottle filled with an amber liquid. "This should help settle your nerves." Wilkerson grinned triumphantly. He handed the small bottle over to Winona.

"What does it do?" she asked.

"I call it the Pacifier. A few sips of that and you won't feel a thing! Nervousness begone. Butterflies in your stomach? Not with Tobias Wilkerson's *'Special Soothing Pacifier.'*"

"All right, save the sales pitch," Jesse said. "This isn't like your other tonic is it, Tobias?"

"Whatever do you mean?"

"Does this one *actually* work?"

Wilkerson hushed Jesse. "Would you keep your voice down? I'd like to make a sale today, and I don't need you spouting falsities like that. And, as a matter of fact, it does work. I've had many satisfied customers with this before."

Jesse eyed the peddler skeptically.

Winona was much more accepting. "Thank you, Tobias! I'll have a sip before we get on."

"You're welcome." Wilkerson climbed back up onto his wagon and took the reins of his horses. "Just a sip, though. A little too much and you'll be sleeping for a good while."

"Tobias, what about Winona's luggage?"

"Don't you worry. I'll have it sent down to the station. It'll be there before you are! Now, if you'll excuse me, a man must make a living!" Tobias snapped the reins and bid farewell to them. Jesse and Winona waved him off before turning to each other.

"Now, what d'you say we go catch us a train?" Jesse said.

WALKING THROUGH TOWN, his arm looped through Winona's, was a pleasant experience. The bustle and noise of the streets were a striking contrast to the ghostly roads of Fortune. People passed them tipping their hats and saying their greetings. They went by a store with its windows full of produce, and another displaying firearms. A teenage boy stood on one corner, grubby and shivering in the cool of the autumn afternoon, as he tried his best to sell copies of the local news sheet.

They rounded a corner, coming off Main Street, and headed up a side road toward the station. The ticket house stood a hundred yards or so ahead of them. Plenty of people were flocking to it, carrying cases or dragging trunks. Just like them, many of them looking to move on, or start anew. Jesse wondered how many of the men were leaving behind California Widows.

Something hit him in the side, and he felt an intense pain in his ribs. He gasped in pain and stumbled against Winona, who almost fell into the mud. He steadied himself and looked down to see a young boy.

The kid was surely no older than ten. Tall for his age, as his head had just butted Jesse's rib cage, but a scrawny-looking kid for his size. His face was tanned but gaunt, scuffed, and marked with long-dried mud. His hair was dark and uneven like it had been cut with a knife. The kid's pale blue shirt was mottled with stains and blotches, and his frayed cotton suspenders held up his baggy brown trousers (holes in those, too). The kid looked up at him with big buggy eyes from a face that was far too thin for a child.

"Sorry," he said and quickly darted away. Jesse went to say something back, but the boy was swallowed up by the crowd.

"Jesse? Are you all right?"

He looked over at Winona. "Yeah," Jesse lied. It hurt to breathe again. "Are you okay?"

"I'm fine for a bit of mud, but're you sure you are? Y'all lookin' like you've seen a ghost."

"No . . . it's nothing," Jesse said, shaking his head. He took her arm in his again and started towards the station again. "Just that kid looked like he could use a good meal is all."

They entered the ticket office, and Jesse was grateful for more steady ground. Across from the entrance were several ticket booths protected by iron bars, from each of which stood lengthy queues of would-be passengers. On one side of the office was a huge blackboard. An attendant was scrawling with chalk at the bottom of it, adding to the list of departures and arrivals for that day.

Jesse wondered how they managed to keep track and organize so many trains coming in and out of one place, let alone have them do it on time. He'd not traveled by train himself but knew people who had, and they'd all attested to how efficient they were in their timings. If a train was to leave at a particular time, it was apt to do so.

The man in front of them, in his khaki frock coat and pecan gambler hat, turned around briefly, smiled at the two of them, and swiftly turned around again. Jesse noted the finery of his garments and the contrast between them and the scuffed and battered condition of his cavalry boots.

"My, my," said the man, exuding a calm friendliness. "My friend, if you'll pardon me, I have to tell you that your lady here is quite possibly the most beautiful woman I have seen in this whole town. And I have been here for *several* days." He took off his hat, revealing sandy, swept-back hair, a lock of which dropped across his forehead as he bowed slightly to Winona. "Ma'am, may I ask your name?" He smiled, exposing the dimpled cheeks of his boyish face.

Jesse looked over to Winona, who had blushed. "Winona," she said.

"A pleasure to meet you, Winona. A name I shall not forget in a hurry." He turned his attention to Jesse now. "And you, my friend. Who might you be, you lucky sumbitch?"

"Jesse Clayton," he said through gritted teeth.

"Nice to meet you, Jesse. I'm Eddie Bradshaw." He extended his hand and Jesse shook it, squeezing harder than he needed to, a lesson he'd learned from Frank Balfour. "Wow, quite a grip you got there! Nice to see a man who appreciates the town coat, too. Why the darker color, though?"

"I find lighter colors show up the blood easier," Jesse said flatly.

"So, where are you headed, Eddie?" Winona said, trying to break the tension. She slid her hand down to Jesse's and took hold of it, giving it a reassuring squeeze.

"I'm hoping to make a *lot* of money, if I've picked the right train!"

"Next!" came the nasal voice of the woman in the ticket booth.

"That's you, *friend*," Jesse said.

Eddie turned around. "Oh, so it is. Thank you, and have a great journey, both!" Eddie walked up to the counter and talked to the woman. A moment later, he had his ticket and as he left the building, he looked over and gave the two of them a tip of his hat.

As Jesse and Winona strode over to the booth, Winona said, "Jesse Clayton, I did not have you pegged for the jealous type, now."

Before he could answer, the plump woman in the booth pushed up her glasses and asked them bluntly, "Where are you going?"

"What's the easiest route to San Francisco?" Winona asked.

"Hell if I know," the woman said. Winona and Jesse shared a glance. Doubt clouded Winona's eyes.

"Is there a station we can get to from here that will have a route to San Francisco?"

"Look, we're a small station. Best advice I can give ya is to get on a train to Spokane. That's the biggest station closest to ya right now. From there, there's probably a line that'll take ya most o' the way to San Francisco. That's a long trip, though. Expensive, too."

"That's fine," Jesse said and patted his coat pocket.

It didn't feel right.

He dug his hand in there to find it empty.

Oh, hell.

"Next available for Spokane is half past one. Will that do ya?"

Jesse wasn't paying attention. He was running his hands through his other pockets, raking his fingers desperately for any semblance of the missing dollars. Winona nodded and reached into her carry bag then pulled out a few dollars to cover the fare for both their tickets. The woman in the booth handed Winona her change and the two tickets. She asked about her luggage, and the woman told her it had been dropped off at the station. She directed Winona to speak to one of the station officers outside. She took Jesse's arm, and they left the ticket office.

When they got outside, she saw his furrowed brow. "Jesse, what's wrong?"

"The money I had. It's gone."

"What?" Winona's eyes widened.

Jesse patted down his pockets again in a wild hope his money might have magically returned to him. He even checked that his gun was still in its holster. It was. He let out a long sigh and said, "That kid who bumped into us earlier? I don't think it was an accident."

2

THE FRIENDLY HANDS OF BARNEY

This was not exactly the brand-new start Jesse had hoped for; getting to San Francisco penniless was going to be a lot more difficult. He looked at Winona as she walked back to him, having sorted the logistics of her belongings with the train staff. She offered up a pained smile as if sensing his dejection.

"It's fine, Jesse. We got our tickets. I've got some money. We'll just figure out the rest of the way once we get into Spokane." Winona looked around at the sprawl of Rathdrum. "I mean, imagine how big it'll be compared to this place. There'll be work . . . or there's other means."

Jesse squeezed her hand. "I don't want you whorin'."

"God, Jesse, no!" Winona snatched her hand away, her face twisted with dismay. "I meant I could cardsharp."

"You can do that?"

"You bet I can. My daddy taught me, and I'm pretty good at it, too. Frank stopped me playing at the Jewel 'cus of it. If there's enough places in Spokane, I could easily make us some money. We won't exactly be rich, but we won't be bundling up in the wild, either."

"You're just fulla surprises, ain't you?"

They walked onto the platform where their train was waiting. A line of carriages stretched off into the distance. Jesse counted at least eight. Huge boxes of wood and steel, at least fifty feet a car, each sporting big, box windows. Jesse could see the benches inside, plenty of them already taken up by passengers.

Winona's grip on his arm tightened as he stepped toward the train, stopping him. Her free hand was clasped to her chest, and she gnawed at her bottom lip. Looking at the behemoth of wood and metal, he understood her dread. Not that he felt it himself: when you've stared down death as many times as he had, it took a bit more than a big box on wheels to stop him in his tracks.

Jesse stepped back to her and fastened an arm around her waist. "Hey, it'll be just fine. Let's just get on there and sit ourselves down. Won't be long until we're in Spokane."

"It's huge, Jesse. I-I didn't think it'd be this big."

"Big is safe," Jesse said. He gently maneuvered her forward to the car. He had a hand on her back as she climbed the steps inside. She took them slowly, feet coming together on each step like a toddler first climbing a set of stairs.

He eased her into the car. It seemed like pretty much everything was made of timber in there. The floor was encumbered with dust and dried mud, and benches for two lined either side of the narrow walkway. Even the roof was covered with varnished panels. The exception was the cotton curtains hanging in the windows, green and grubby with dirt.

They sidled down, nodding and smiling at the people who peppered the benches, before finding one empty. Jesse sat Winona at the window. "There," he said. "This way, you'll get all the pretty views."

"What about you?" Winona asked.

"I can just look at you."

That brought a smile to her pale face. She reached into her bag and pulled out the tiny bottle of tonic Wilkerson had given her. She popped the cork and upended it into her mouth. Jesse watched on in slight horror, as he saw her neck bob with each swallow. In three, it was empty.

"Whew! That's got a kick to it," Winona said as she wiped her mouth. She popped the cork back before returning it to her purse.

"I'm pretty sure you were just supposed to take a sip," Jesse said.

"Well, Jesse, I'm a bit nervous right now, *okay*? It's a little unsettling getting up inside a giant metal snake on wheels. You may've noticed."

He had. He thought better of saying it out loud, though. Instead, he just put an arm around her and kissed her on the cheek. "I'll keep you safe, don't worry."

"Knowing your luck, this train'll probably get robbed," Winona said, though 'probably' came out a little slurred. That tonic worked fast.

"Last time you were in trouble, I saved you, didn't I?"

"I'm pretty sure I saved myself." Winona's vowels had started to drag.

"The time before that, then. And nobody got shot that time, too."

"But . . . my daddy . . . got hurt."

"Touché."

He could feel her head starting to lull. She shifted herself to lean against the window. Jesse moved his arm away, then helped position hers between her head and the window to make her more comfortable. At least she'd be too busy sleeping to worry for most of the journey. Maybe he'd catch a nap himself.

He watched her for a moment, enjoying the peace on her face as she let her eyes close. He thought about the stroke of luck that had brought them together, saving her life and getting caught up in all that trouble. She'd been worth it. For the first time in years, it felt like he had something worth having. A question suddenly struck him: could it be that his days of wandering were over? He dared to think about settling down with her.

Jesse looked out the window and froze. He saw the boy who'd robbed him on the platform. The scruffy little thief's eyes were shifting side to side, as he stuck his hand into the pocket of an unsuspecting gentleman.

A thought crossed Jesse's mind. He glanced up at the clock overlooking the platform. Ten minutes until the train was due to depart. Plenty of time.

He gently slipped away from Winona, pausing briefly to plant a soft kiss on her head. She smelled of lavender, and it sent a pang of guilt through his gut for leaving her, even for just a few minutes. He rose silently from the bench and then looked around the car. Two rows away sat an old woman, almost swallowed up by the huge broadsheet she was holding.

"Excuse me, ma'am?" Jesse said. The newspaper crinkled down with the flick of a wrist and the woman's head pointed down. Eyes regarded him suspiciously over her thick glasses. "Could you do me a favor? You see my . . ." Jesse paused a moment as he thought about what word to use. He looked back at Winona, wondering. In all the fun of actually being together, they'd never actually come to the point of labeling it. "Friend," he settled on. "She's feeling a little tired is all, and I just need to run a quick errand before we depart." He snatched a look outside again. Thief Boy was still there. "Could you keep an eye on her, please?"

The woman gave a curt nod.

"Thank you!" Jesse said as he walked over to her. "Here's her ticket in case they check before I come back. Thank you again, ma'am."

The old woman took the ticket and returned to her paper. He started down the walkway when she said with a surprisingly authoritative tone, "I'd hurry, young man. You haven't got long."

"Oh, I'll be back," Jesse said, then stepped off the train.

ON THE PLATFORM, he spied the thief again just as he was turning to leave. The kid spotted Jesse and for a moment the two of them locked eyes. The kid's eyes were wide and alert, like an animal in the presence of a predator.

He bolted.

Jesse cursed inwardly as the young boy took off running down the platform. Jesse went off in pursuit. The boy rounded the ticket office;

Jesse did too a moment later and had to act fast in order to avoid clattering a young woman and her baby. He whirled around them as the woman squealed. Jesse shook off the brief dizziness of his spin, and he carried on sprinting through the crowded street.

The kid ducked down an alley and Jesse followed. It was narrow and it stank, every step bringing up splashes of rank water. The kid sidestepped down another alley. Jesse's lungs were starting to burn with each breath. The distance between the two of them was starting to grow as well.

The boy turned out onto the main street and scrabbled under a horse, ignoring the protests of its rider. Jesse took the long way around it and caught the shoulder of a passerby. Jesse stumbled and found his footing, but the other man did not, hitting the muck face first and screaming expletives at him. Jesse called back an apology as he carried on. His legs were starting to complain now, too.

The thief had nipped into another alleyway, but when Jesse followed him into it, he skidded to a halt, his boots digging grooves through the sludge. The alley was a dead end, backing onto the back wall of another building. Jesse paced to the wall. He looked around. He saw the thief squeezing his way like a rodent through the space between the buildings. There was no way Jesse could fit through.

He put his hands on his hips, blew out a sigh, and then stood a moment to catch his breath. He had to hand it to the kid. He was good and he was fast. He was sharp, too. Jesse accepted the defeat and waited for his heavy breathing to settle. As he started to make his way back down the alleyway, he heard a scream.

The scream of a young boy.

JESSE RAN AGAIN, making his best guess at where that scream had come from. He rounded the building. On the other side, Jesse saw another dingy alleyway where the scream had come from. The kid had been going in that direction, too.

The alley led into a space between a saloon and a neighboring structure. A stack of barrels stood against the back wall of the saloon and a rough stack of broken crates gathered in one corner. Next to that was the young thief, his collar in the grasp of a very angry-looking man with a handlebar mustache. It looked like this boy's luck had run out.

"Where's my money, ya little turd? You tell me now!" the man growled. He shook the boy as his little legs dangled helplessly.

"I ain't got nothin', mister. I swear I ain't the one done robbed you. On my momma."

The boy wailed as the man slammed him into the wall. "I ain't havin' it. I saw what you did!"

"All right now, friend, that's enough," Jesse said, making himself known as he saw no need to hurt the kid. "I think the boy gets the message.

Why don't you just drop him down in the mud there and I'm sure he'll be more'n happy to oblige your request."

Handlebar turned Jesse's way with a snarl. "What're you, his daddy?"

"I'm here for the same reason as you."

"Then allow me to help," Handlebar said and grinned as he slammed the kid into the wall again. The boy screeched. The man was by no means gentle.

"You keep doing that, you'll break him. He's no use to us then."

"Then I can just *take* my money back."

"And if he doesn't have it on him?"

Handlebar paused for a second, considering. That second dragged out into several, and Jesse remembered how he'd already burned a fair bit of time chasing down the kid. He couldn't wait for this guy's brain to catch up with the rest of the world. Eventually, he let go of the kid's collar and the poor boy plopped into the mud. He grimaced and rubbed at his back as he gingerly rose to his feet.

Jesse stepped over to them now. "Come on, kid. Hand us what's ours and you have my word, no more harm'll come to you," Jesse said. The boy looked up at him, trying his best to keep back the tears and project his meanest scowl—an eggshell mask at best. "Anything else but that happens in the next few seconds, and I'll leave you in the friendly hands of Mr. Handlebar Mustache here."

"Mr. *What*?" Handlebar protested.

Jesse turned to him. "I'm sorry, I didn't catch your name."

"It's Barney."

Jesse gave him a thumbs-up and then he turned back to the boy. "I'll leave you in the friendly hands of Barney here." Then, to Barney, "That better?"

Barney nodded.

"What'll it be, kid?" Jesse asked. The boy's eyes darted between the two of them and then around the alley. Jesse could see what he was up to and said, "Come on now, don't be stupid. You go and run, you won't get far." He rested his hand on the butt of his Colt. Barney cracked his knuckles.

The rigidness in the boy deflated and his shoulders sunk. He dug his hands into his pockets and offered up two wads of cash. Jesse took his, still clasped in a silver money clip. Barney took his crumpled dollars and huffed.

"You're lucky this guy was here, kid," Barney said and then stomped away.

Jesse watched Barney as he left the alley, waiting until he was out of sight before he started talking. "He's right," Jesse said, turning back to the kid with a sympathetic smile. "What's your name, kid?"

"What do you care?"

"I'd like to know the name of the person that just robbed me."

"Henry Pye. Happy now?" The kid folded his arms. He was petulant. His voice wasn't quite deep enough to carry the hard-ass attitude he was trying so hard for, though.

"Nice to meet you, Henry Pye. I'm Jesse Clayton."

"Good for you," Henry said flatly. Jesse couldn't help but find the kid funny. He'd seen this attitude before, kids out there with nobody to look out for them but themselves. To have the gall to give attitude to the man with a gun he'd just robbed was to be commended. Until the likely day that he did it to the wrong man.

Jesse fished a dollar out of his money clip. "Here, take this. Get yourself some food. You look hungry."

The thief eyed the dollar and then Jesse suspiciously. "Why? I just robbed you. Most folks'd give me a beating, then send me on my way. Why would you gimme a dollar?"

"I'm not most folks. Maybe I know what it's like to be a young kid on the street," Jesse said. The boy snatched the dollar and then scampered off back the way he'd come into the alley.

In the distance, Jesse heard the high-pitched squeal of a whistle. A moment after that there came the deeper, louder *CHOO!* of a much *bigger* whistle. A moment after that followed the deep chugging of a steam engine and the thumping of the initial throes of lugging its load of rail cars.

Oh, hell.

Jesse ran back out into the street. He looked around for a clock, hoping that somehow, he wasn't going to see what he expected to see. He spotted one hanging above the bank of Rathdrum. He grimaced as he saw the time.

Thirty minutes past one.

3

SELL ME ON SUNDAY

Jesse rubbed at his chin, the stubble prickling his palm. He'd still tried to catch the train, sprinting to the station in the hope that it had somehow been delayed despite what he'd heard. Sure enough, when he arrived at the platform it was empty. In the distance, he saw the metallic snake slithering away with Winona in its belly, a plume of smoke slinking in the sky above it.

Still watching it go, he mulled things over in his head. Frustrating as it was, it was not the end of the world. No need to panic. Yes, Winona would be angry enough to pitch a fit when she woke up, but there was nothing to be done about that. Besides, it would be a fun story to tell one day. That he was sure of.

Jesse figured he'd just catch the next train (whenever that was) and get word to Winona for when she reached Spokane that he would meet her there . . . just later. He'd make it up to her; he had his money back. If anything, it was a blessing in disguise. They wouldn't need to stay in Spokane to raise the funds to journey on.

Jesse had convinced himself. That was the easy part. The hard part would be convincing Winona. They'd not been apart in days, and the one moment when she needed him, he'd left her sleeping in the belly of a beast she found terrifying.

At least he had a good while to work on his apology.

IN A BIT of luck that had gone Jesse's way, two things had sprung up rather fortuitously for him. The first was that the next train to Spokane was at two o'clock. The second was that Rathdrum had a Western Union, and it was situated right next to the train station.

After a short wait in line, he'd managed to get a telegram sent to the Spokane station (It amazed him how that message was already there only minutes later, waiting for Winona, who would not be for another few hours.) informing her of his apology, delay, and expected arrival. He couldn't go into detail; a telegram was paid for per letter. Being that fast meant it wasn't that cheap.

By the time he got back to the platform, the two o'clock train was already waiting and filling up with passengers. This one was a little smaller; Jesse counted only five cars attached to the locomotive. The last car seemed to be just for luggage, as he saw a group of train staff loading up a pile of suitcases and boxes onto it.

Something caught Jesse's attention. Familiar colors in a khaki town coat and pecan hat. He saw Eddie talking with three other men. He shook each of their hands before they broke up and peeled away into the gathering mass queuing for the train cars. Through the people, Eddie caught sight of Jesse and bid him a tilt of his hat, which Jesse returned.

Jesse got on the last of the passenger cars at the rear of the train.

Upkeep of cars was apparently not a priority for Union Pacific as this car was in an even worse state than the one Winona was currently sleeping in. Several of the curtains were torn, and the floor was patchy with mud, dust, and grit. The benches were chipped and scuffed. One was so badly damaged it looked likely to splinter a man.

Jesse took the next bench down across from an old-timer with weedy, white hair crawling out from under his bowler hat. Jesse sat down and smiled at the man. The old-timer returned a glare, eyes narrowed to slits, his face leathered, and his nose reddened and bulbous. A sign of a penchant for alcohol. He had himself a gun, too. Jesse thought it to be a Smith and Wesson hanging from his right hip. A fine weapon to have. Jesse wondered why a man like him would need it.

The car was filling up and the train was due to leave in a couple of minutes. A woman stepped into the car and stood at the end, her eyes scanning the benches. Her eyes settled on Jesse, and he looked around the car. Plenty of the benches were filled. Only a few had spaces, apparently, Jesse looked the least threatening of the potential seating partners as she strode down toward him.

Her twill walking skirt swished with every step, and she kept her head bowed, shaded by the black bonnet that swallowed up her chestnut hair. Her coat was folded over her arm, and as he stood up to let her have the window seat, he noted the floral embroidery and high collar of her Darlington blouse.

He sat down next to her. She was all folded in on herself, knees tucked together, arms folded over her coat. Guarded and rigid. She gave Jesse a swift, sheepish glance as she thanked him. In that glimpse, he saw a woman older than his twenty-five years for sure, and by a few years. She had a rounded face and deep bags under her eyes. The right cheek was slightly yellowed, an almost-healing bruise perhaps. She was all nerves.

Sitting next to a stranger wasn't going to help.

After the whistle from the controller, and the deep *choo!* of the train, Jesse felt the tug as it lurched and then steadily crawled along the tracks. Slowly, the station was left behind. Soon, the train picked up speed as luscious views of the country began to rush by.

"Hi, there," he said. "I'm Jesse Clayton."

The woman concerned herself with the view.

"What are you heading to Spokane for?" Jesse tried again. The woman's head moved, ever so slightly, away from the window.

"A fresh start," she said in a sad whisper.

"Really?" Jesse tried to sound as jovial and non-threatening as he could. He kept his hand over his coat to make sure it continued to conceal his gun. No need to make this lady any more uneasy. This was a long trip; he'd rather have a bit of conversation to help pass it by a little swifter. "You know, I'm fitting to find the same thing. Although it's not exactly gotten off to the best start. I was supposed to be on a train with my . . ." There it was again, that label they didn't have. ". . . friend." It still didn't sound right, but for now, it would suffice.

She turned her head away from the window and gave him a brief smile, then returned her attention to the passing pine trees.

"When she wakes up, I'm gonna be in real trouble."

"Your friend." She said the word with enough weight as if she understood it was more than that. "Did you upset her?"

"No. Not exactly. Well, not yet anyway. She was scared of taking a trip on a train, it being her first time and all, had a little too much tonic and fell asleep," Jesse rambled.

"And you left her?"

"Yeah. Well, that's kind of complicated. You see I was robbed and . . . I did send a message ahead and—"

"I wouldn't worry," she said, turning to him fully now. She smiled weakly at him, and he could see the fullness of her face. She was much older than him; the crow's feet perched on her eyes gave that away. She looked tired, like she'd been carrying a heavy burden of fear or guilt. Maybe both. Jesse thought to ask about it. Getting a better look at that yellow cheek too, he was sure that was the last remnants of a bruise almost healed. "You may have made a mistake, but you've the thoughtfulness to rectify it as best you can. Not many men would do that."

"Well, you've made me feel plenty better, thank you . . ." Jesse trailed off, hoping for a name.

"Irene Berg."

"It's lovely to make your acquaintance, Irene. And thank you for putting a fool's mind at ease." He tried to think of a way to ask what was wrong without asking. "What does your fresh start look like, Irene?" Jesse asked, keeping up the jovial tone.

"Mr. Clayton, I—"

"Jesse, please."

"I'm not sure I wish to tell my personal business to a man I've just met." She glanced back at the window. He was losing her.

"Well, how about If I share a bit about me first? You get to know me, then I you?" Jesse gestured to the car around them. "I got nowhere to go and it's a long trip."

"Thank you, really, but *please*, leave me to myself, Mr. Clayton."

Jesse nodded. "Of course. I'm sorry, Mrs. Berg."

"*Miss* Berg." She turned back to the window.

"I'm sorry, Miss Berg," Jesse said. Inwardly, he cursed himself. Had Winona been there the two of them would have been hollering by now. Talking came easy to Winona; no matter who you were she could strike up a conversation about something, anything. She could probably even get a laugh out of a stone. She just had that about her. Jesse was suddenly aware of how much he missed her and felt a stab of guilt in his belly at leaving her alone.

Instead of watching her sleep off her worries, here he was playing a lone hand in a train car full of strangers, while she slept off the trip miles farther along this very track. Was that irony? Jesse couldn't tell.

Jesse wasn't smart enough for that.

"Clayton. Clayton. Hmm. *Clayton*." The old man to his left was looking at Jesse now, saying his name. "Well, pickle me in vinegar and sell me on Sunday." The old-timer flashed him a grin full of yellowing teeth. "You're the man who put Slim Joe in the ground, ain'tcha?"

"I might could be," Jesse said. More accurately, he was the man who was almost drowned in mud by Slim Joe Cullen. Frank Balfour was technically the man who killed him when he shot him, and they'd left him to die at the old Mabin mine. The old-timer didn't need details, though.

"Fine work there, son. He's crossed paths with us on more'n one occasion." His voice was coarse and wheezy. He probably enjoyed a cigarette, too. "Never been able to put him in the ground, though." The old-timer chuckled. He pulled out a hip flask, unscrewing it as he talked. "He go down easy, or he make you work for it?"

For a second, Jesse felt the mud in his ears and his mouth again.

"He put up a fight, yeah," Jesse said.

"Congratulations on that one. Him and his boys had caused enough trouble round these parts in recent years. Especially in that little town of Fortify."

"*Fortune*," Jesse corrected. He was surprised at how much that comment had needled him. He'd taken quite a liking to that town.

"Yes, yes, that's the one." The old-timer took a pull of his flask. He grimaced as it went down. "Never understood why they didn't hire us to sort the problem."

If I wanted to waste my money, I'd wheel it down to Cullen now and save us all a lot of trouble.

Frank's words echoed in Jesse's head. "You're a Pinkerton."

"Pinkerton *detective*," the old-timer corrected now. "Pinkerton agent Milton Phelps, at your service," Phelps said. He then pulled back the lapel of his jacket with grubby fingers, nails black with dirt. Pinned to the inside of it was a shield-shaped steel badge. PINKERTON NATIONAL DETECTIVE AGENCY was engraved into it. It didn't shine, and it looked as dingy as the man who wore it. Phelps pulled his hand away, now with a triumphant smile adorned on his face, clearly quite impressed with himself.

Well, that makes one of us.

"My job here is to keep these folks safe, should anything untoward happen." Phelps's words rolled out thick and sticky with arrogance. Jesse had to quell an urge to hit the smug son of a bitch.

Instead of throwing up his fists, Jesse just humored Phelps with a nod. Pinkertons weren't on trains to keep the people safe. That wasn't how they worked, not in Jesse's experiences with them, at least. Pinkertons were little more than guns for hire and Pinkertons did whatever the money told 'em to do. The ones Jesse had come across weren't much bullet, either. Just as apt to take a bribe and turn a blind eye as they were to actually do their jobs.

But Phelps being on this train meant two things: the first was that he wouldn't be alone; agents often came in twos. The second was that his presence meant there was either money or something worth a lot of it on this train, and that was what warranted their protection. It also meant there were either agents or marshals at Spokane, too. Hell, there had probably been a handful keeping an eye on the train while it was in Rathdrum, too.

"Well, I sure feel a lot safer knowing you're on board, Detective," Jesse said, forcing himself to smile too. What else could he say?

He didn't need to say anything else, as the car door opened and for a brief moment the rushing of the wind drew both their attention. The woman closing the door then held onto that attention.

Fiery auburn hair tumbled around her porcelain face. High cheekbones, full lips reddened by lipstick, and a fair complexion gave her a doll-like look. She wore a caramel faux suede vest over a shirt and brown canvas pants that held tight enough to show her womanly figure. It was attire Jesse didn't often see on a woman.

He didn't often see one looking this terrified either.

"Help! Please!" she cried, putting a hand to her mouth. "I think this train is being robbed!"

4

A TIN BADGE AND A GUN

The train started to slow down. Jesse could feel it. That subtle force pulling him into the bench, generated by the train's motion, was steadily diminishing. He glanced at Irene, whose pallid face was now a mask of worry. The woman with the auburn hair stepped away from the door, her knee-high leather boots clunking along the walkway.

Phelps stood up and flashed her his badge. *Subtle*, Jesse thought.

"Just what do you mean, ma'am?" he said.

Her face lit up when she saw his badge, and she took her hand away from her mouth. "Oh, thank my stars, a lawman! They're robbin' this train!" the lady drawled. She was from the South, that was for sure.

"Okay," Phelps said and beckoned her over. "Come here and tell me what ya can." As she moved to the bench, the train jostled and she stumbled into it, grabbing Phelps's collar on the way down. As she let go, she left a red smudge of her lipstick behind.

"Oh, my, I'm sorry I musta got it on my hands and—"

"Pay it no mind. It's a damned shirt. Now tell me, missy, what's yer name?"

"Roxie."

"Okay, Roxie, tell me just how many you saw setting themselves to rob this here train."

Jesse took a moment to lean into the walkway, looking down and through the window of the door. He couldn't see much in the next car: the lighting was poor and the glass was fogged. *Somebody should open up a window*, he thought.

"I saw two of them, but there might be more, I ain't sure. I heard 'em shoutin' in the next car from mine so I up and just got out, not thinkin' there's nowhere else to go on a train." Roxie laughed nervously.

"It's all right, you just sit here and calm yourself down. When they come here—which they will—I'll be ready for 'em. They won't be robbin' nobody on this train, not today. Not while Pinkerton detective Milton Phelps is alive." He took another pull of his hip flask, then slid it into his pocket.

Nothing about what Jesse had just seen was reassuring.

Phelps let Roxie slide across to the window seat, then sat down in his new position, one leg out in the walkway. He pulled out his gun (Indeed, it was a Smith and Wesson, a fine weapon to waste on a fella like him.) and he held it in his lap. His face steeled as he focused his attention on the door of the train car.

The train rocked back as it came to a dead stop. People started to murmur, and an air of concern hung in the car.

"Listen up, folks," Phelps addressed the rest of the passengers, his voice dropping an octave with authority. "Y'all just need to stay in your seats, and you'll be absolutely fine. I'll handle this."

Jesse glanced at Irene. She looked about as reassured as he was.

"Clayton," Phelps whispered as he leaned over. Jesse caught the stiff smell of whiskey. "You good to back me up?"

"Why would I wanna go and risk my life for somebody else's money?" Jesse whispered back.

"Because I'm deputizin' ya, that's why."

"That might work on your friends, but you ain't a marshal. You're a hired hand with a tin badge and a gun. You can't deputize me, Milton."

The old-timer huffed. "I can see to it that you'll be paid. A more than fair price too. All we gotta do is unload on them once they close that there door. We can drop 'em before they know what's hit them."

There were a few holes to poke in that. The first being the assumption that they would close the door. All sorts of things could go wrong. Plenty of variables to be considered. They had next-to-no cover; if the would-be train robbers simply opened fire at any point, they'd be torn apart by bullets along with the crappy wooden benches and the other passengers. Nope, it was not the smart play to sit and wait for it. They needed to get up and take the fight to them.

"No, Milton, this is what—"

The car door opened.

Oh, hell.

In stepped Eddie Bradshaw, brandishing a Colt in either hand, their barrels sweeping across the passengers. Behind him, Jesse recognized one of the gentlemen Eddie had been conversing with on the platform. There had been the four of them altogether, Jesse recalled, so at the very least there were two others to come.

Eddie's friend was taller, wider in his frame, having to slip through into the car sideways, minding the huge bag slung over his shoulder. Jesse caught sight of his face beneath the brim of his hat; a bristly beard settled beneath his jaw, while his face was covered in patches of lumpy, white skin. The kind of scarring a man can get from a flame. It brought back memories of the Jewel ablaze.

The man on fire falling from the balcony.

Christie.

Jesse banished the thought from his mind. He couldn't afford distractions right now. He had a gun pointed at him and he was sitting next to a drunken liability. Eddie was scanning the room when his eyes and both of his Colts settled their attention on Milton. He walked over to the Pinkerton.

"Well, good afternoon, Detective," Eddie said and swiped the butt of his pistol across Phelps's head.

Phelps flung back into the bench and his head lolled. Roxie screamed and pressed herself against the window. Phelps cried out in pain, his Smith and Wesson slipped from his lap to the floor as he slumped down, a glazed look in his eyes. Blood began to ooze from a cut above his left eyebrow.

Eddie waved the guns around again. "Nobody do anything stupid, please. And if anybody else here is either a Pinkerton or is currently in possession of a gun, please raise your hand—empty, that is—so that my colleague here, Mr. Wood, can relieve you of it."

Phelps regarded Eddie with wide eyes as blood continued to seep down his cheek. Roxie kept herself pressed to the window, wide-eyed and open-mouthed.

Jesse didn't have much of a choice. Sure, he was fast on the draw, but not fast enough to move his coat, pull and clear the bench, then aim before Eddie Bradshaw could move two inches to his left and pull both triggers. This was not the time to get himself killed.

Jesse raised his hand.

Eddie cocked his head quizzically. "My, my, Jesse, is that you? What a delight it is to see you and your lady . . . oh." Eddie paused when he looked at Irene sitting next to him. "Your tastes sure have changed since our initial meeting, my friend."

"Winona caught an earlier train. Right now, I'm pretty glad she did."

Eddie looked down at his guns and twisted them in his hands as he frowned playfully. "Yeah, sorry about this. But none of y'all need to worry, now. We're not here to rob any of you."

"Is that so?"

"Absolutely. All you gotta do is stay in your seats until we're done. Now lift up your piece, nice and slow. I hear you even brush that hammer . . . you're a dead man, my friend."

Jesse obeyed, slipping his hand down and pulling out his Colt. Finger in the trigger guard, he spun it and caught it by the barrel. He then extended the wood-finished butt to Eddie.

Mr. Wood reached over and snatched it out of his hand, tucking it into his bandolier.

"I'll be sure to leave your iron on the train, too. A fine piece it is," Bradshaw said.

"That's real kind. But if you ain't here to rob us, who are you here to rob?"

Eddie gave Jesse a friendly nudge with his elbow. "You don't need to worry about that now, my friend. Just sit tight and it'll all be over soon, and you and everyone here will be on your way."

Eddie's gaze darted up and out the window. Jesse followed to see a man drop from a window in the next car. He nervously glanced back before taking off at a sprint across the dirt. He got about twelve yards before the was a sharp *crack!* and the man pitched forward into the ground. He writhed in the dirt for a moment, then lay still.

"Take note," Eddie said. "What happens when y'all try to leave your seats."

Farther down the track came a figure all in black. He walked to the front of the train, disappearing from view.

"Excellent. Looks like Mateo has done his job. We'll be on our way again shortly, ladies and gentlemen." Eddie turned to his associate. "We can continue with the job, Mr. Wood."

Wood nodded. Like Big Dan, he was a man of few words.

Eddie walked to the rear of the car and Mr. Wood followed. As he passed Phelps, he grabbed the man's gun and then the man by the collar. Phelps let out a holler as he was dragged down the train. Jesse watched as the three of them disappeared through the door into the luggage storage car.

Whatever it was they were here to rob, it had to be in there. Safes most likely, or a private car for some wealthy and unlucky fellow about to have an unsanctioned withdrawal.

Something about this robbery didn't feel right. Jesse just couldn't put his finger on it yet. Maybe it was just Eddie being too damned friendly for a man robbing a train. Clearly, these boys had a plan in place, but why was the man so laid back?

The train lurched and then carried forward again. Jesse felt it pull to the right, and he looked out of the window to see that instead of carrying on straight, the train was now diverging onto another track. So, Mateo's job was to switch up the track and grab the horses. That wasn't good. He could feel it in his gut.

Nobody pulls a train off course if they have honorable intentions. What were they gonna do? Dump it and them miles out in the middle of nowhere? *Hell, was this sister track even finished?* Depending on how far off they got, it could be hours or even days before they'd be found. Whatever was in that storage car had to be of serious value if they were willing to go to these extreme lengths.

That meant Jesse couldn't let them finish the job. Otherwise, he, Roxie, Irene, and all these other passengers had bought themselves a one-way ticket to ruin. He had to get back to Winona. He wasn't about to let himself or anyone else die for being unlucky enough to board the wrong train.

He was outnumbered. They had his weapon. The one man who may have been helpful had just been dragged away bleeding, most likely minutes away from death. He had nowhere to go without running into them.

But he wasn't unarmed.

For the next time you lose your gun.

Frank's words were in his head again as Jesse slid his hand down to his boot and fingered the thin wooden handle tucked into it.

Jesse had a knife.

Jesse had time.

All he needed now was a plan.

5

STEEL STRIKING STEEL

Jesse glanced around at all the sullen faces in the silent train car. Shocked and adorned with fear, none of them would be much help to him. As long as they didn't get in the way, that was all right. He wasn't about to have any innocents get caught in the crossfire. Not again. Jesse looked up and down the car, seeing it was clear, and started to get up.

A hand shot out and seized his arm.

"What are you doing?" Irene's stressed whisper came at him like a dagger. Her tired eyes were wide and alert now, bloodshot and scared. "You heard what the man said. You'll get yourself killed."

Jesse put a hand on hers and gently lifted it away. "Irene, I appreciate your concern. I'm just gonna try and take a look around. Get a better sense of my bearings."

"Get us all shot is more like what you'll do," a man called out from across the car.

"Keep your voice down," Jesse said, minding to keep his low, too. "You let me worry about getting myself shot. You all just stay in your seats like the man said and you won't have to worry. I'm just terrible at keeping still."

As he stepped into the walkway, he shot Roxie a reassuring smile. Her lips curled slightly but her eyes were still wrought.

The train jostled and Jesse had to steady himself on a bench. It was then he realized the train was traveling much faster than it had been before it had stopped. Another cause for concern. Any train that traveled too quickly was at risk of derailing.

There was no use going backward; Jesse assumed Eddie and his friend would be occupied for a while as they attempted to get at the spoils they sought. Forward unto the front was his bearing, then. If he could get to the engine, he could try and stop it. That would remove the risk of derailment while giving the robbers a reason to move to the front of the train and away from the passengers.

The first order of business was removing the threats of the two armed men ahead of him.

Jesse withdrew the blade from his boot and held it pointed down, tucking it parallel to his wrist. No need to brandish a knife in front of already terrified passengers.

He opened the car door, hearing the rush of the passing wind as he stepped onto the gangway outside. The gap between the cars was only a few feet, bracketed by iron railings to prevent falling. Jesse could see the couplers beneath, jostling in their embrace. He also noted a ladder to the side of the door, an alternate means of crossing the car should it be occupied.

Jesse crossed to the next car, keeping low and out of sight of the window. He looked inside and couldn't see anybody prowling the walkway. This car wasn't as packed as his was. Jesse opened the door and slipped inside. Immediately, a dozen pairs of eyes snapped to him. He put a finger to his lips and swiftly made his way along the length of the car.

People whispered at him as he moved by them. He heard their hushed and panicked exclamations.

"What are you doing?"

"—Are you mad?"

"—The hell are you doin', son?"

"—You fixin' to die?"

"—Yer crazy, you odd fish!"

He waved them off, instead carrying on in determined, quiet strides along the train car. He was grateful that was the only confrontation so far. He still had three other cars to get through. He was bound to run into more deadly opposition sooner or later. What would he do when faced with a gun?

I'll cross that bridge when I get to it.

The gangway was clear. Jesse opened the rail car door and stepped outside into the familiar whoosh of the onrushing air. The train was cutting through plains now, great swaths of green on either side of him flying by in a blur. He took a moment to take a breath, feeling his accelerated heart rate. He felt the adrenaline just waiting to surge into his system. The anticipation of the inevitable confrontation reminded him of when he was a child; he and his brother would spend their days playing hide and seek in the trees until their mother would call them for supper.

His mother. Thinking about her reminded him of the note he carried.

Missoula wasn't too far from here, you know.

He shook away the thought. He didn't have time to daydream. He looked up at the window of the door to the next rail car as he reached for the handle. A man was staring back at him. Dressed all in black, olive-colored skin, patchy black stubble, and a grizzly, knotted scar lined from one cheek across his nose to the other.

Jesse had found Mateo.

THE HANDLE of the door jerked, and Mateo shouldered into it, knocking Jesse back into the gangway. Jesse heard the shouts and squeals of the passengers behind Mateo as he brought up his short double-barreled shotgun.

Jesse lunged at Mateo, slamming him back against the door and slamming it shut. Mateo's cracking impact spider-webbed the glass. Jesse slammed Mateo's wrist against the rail. The Mexican cried out and lost his grip on the scattergun. It fell beneath the train, lost in the howl of the onrushing wind.

Jesse brought up his blade. He darted forward and jabbed for Mateo's stomach, but the wiry man stepped to his right and slashed down with his hand, chopping Jesse's wrist and knocking it away. He followed that blow-up by throwing his gloved left fist into Jesse's face. Jesse ducked, narrowly avoiding the blow that would have broken his nose.

Jesse took a step back, bringing up the knife again. He gave his wrist a shake, the blood inside buzzing after Mateo's viper-like blow. He couldn't retreat too far; he had to stay close to prevent Mateo from drawing his gun. If he did, it was all over for Jesse.

"Mateo, right?" Jesse said.

"Si," came Mateo's reply.

This wasn't like the Cullen fight. Jesse had been vastly overpowered in that encounter and thrown around like a ragdoll. Though here it was *very* close quarters, Jesse fancied his chances against Mateo. Jesse had the blade and therefore the advantage. While Mateo was quick, one clean strike would end it. He could whittle the Mexican down with slashes to arms and legs, though time was not on Jesse's side. If he wasted too much, he left himself vulnerable to Eddie and his friend once they finished their business.

Mateo grabbed either side of his silver belt buckle and pulled. Out came a pair of push daggers. He nestled the handles in his palms, the blades protruding through his fingers.

So much for the advantage.

Mateo drove forward, jabbing with his right hand. Jesse ducked and swiped with his blade. It caught Mateo's shirt, leaving a gash in the fabric and nothing else. He countered with his other hand, driving down, and Jesse had to think fast. He grabbed the man's wrist, stopping the blade inches from his eye, and threw it up in the air. Rising himself, he drove a boot into Mateo, knocking him back.

Jesse wanted to catch his breath, his lungs starting to itch from his exertions, but Jesse knew he had to press forward while his attacker was off balance. Jesse stepped forward and immediately realized his mistake. Mateo smirked as he instantly steadied himself and then flicked his right hand. The push dagger sailed through the air. Jesse stooped and felt the blade nick his Stetson. Mateo brought his boot up with force, cracking Jesse on the jaw. He felt a dizzying light-headedness. Jesse fell on his ass and then his back. His head hit the steel, knocking his hat off.

That mistake was about to cost him dearly.

Mateo stood over him, then knelt and straddled him. It was a scene that felt all too familiar, only this time Frank wasn't around with a Winchester to pick him off with a well-placed shot in the back.

Jesse waited for his vision to settle as the Mexican mumbled in Spanish. Jesse's dancing eyesight steadied, and he saw Mateo clasp his hands together and lean forward, readying to drive the remaining push dagger down. His hands plunged as Jesse's right forearm shot up, catching the interlocked fists and deflecting the blow. Knocked off balance, Mateo shoved the blade into the gangway and Jesse heard the whining scrape of steel striking steel.

Seizing the opportunity, Jesse ran his knife into Mateo's stomach. The Mexican gasped and jolted as the blade slipped into his skin. Jesse gritted his teeth and twisted the blade. Mateo grunted and jerked as he felt the tearing of his flesh. The push blade clattered on the steel of the gangway. Jesse felt warmth as Mateo's blood ran down the blade and onto his clenched fist.

Jesse pushed the dying Mateo away and slumped on the metal next to him. Mateo's breathing became hard and ragged. He moved his hands down and pressed them into his stomach. Jesse saw the silver necklace that had fallen out of his shirt: a crucifix, the base of it now doused in blood. Mateo was mumbling again. Jesse guessed he was making his peace with God.

Jesse pushed himself up onto his knees and then used the railing to stand up, before resting on it to catch his breath. He winced as his forearm touched the railing and he pulled it away. Through the fresh slit in his coat and shirt, Jesse saw that he had a deep gash a few inches long from where he'd blocked Mateo's last attack.

Damn, those push daggers were sharp.

Out of the corner of his eye, he sensed movement. Jesse turned just in time to see Mateo, blood dripping from his lips, one hand on his wound, lunging for him. Jesse broke away from the railing just in time as Mateo slammed into it. He cried out in pain. He started to turn but Jesse grabbed the back of Mateo's collar and his belt and lifted him up and over the railing. Mateo's scream was cut off when he went under the train. Jesse winced as he felt a bump reverberate through the car.

Jesse bent over, placing his hands on his knees as he took in a deep lungful of air. Inwardly, he cursed as he realized he'd just tossed Mateo's gun over the railing along with him. He reached down, picking up the push dagger his would-be assassin had dropped and tucked into his belt. It was better than nothing, he guessed. He picked up his Stetson too, placing it back on his head with aplomb.

Jesse opened the door to the next car and went inside.

6

A POWERFUL BEAST INDEED

The passengers all regarded him with the same look of stunned astonishment. Jesse closed the door and walked through. He had an uncanny sense of déjà vu as he did; each set of eyes tracked his movement along the train car.

"Did you . . . did you kill that guy?" a man to his left said, his jowls wobbling with each word.

"It was either him or me," Jesse replied.

"Are you okay?" a young woman to Jesse's right asked. He nodded to her and gave her a smile he hoped was more convincing than it felt.

"What about the others?" the old woman next to her said from behind her big canvas bag.

"I've only dealt with the one so far, ma'am. I'm not quite that quick."

The old woman frowned at him.

Jesse shrugged. "You're welcome to come take on the next one with me." The old woman found the passing views suddenly very interesting. Another duel won by Jesse Clayton, this one considerably easier than the last. He moved on, reaching the end of the car, where he peeked through the window to the gangway and the final passenger car ahead. He savored the rush of the outside air as he stepped out and crossed to the last car. A quick peek inside told him it was clear, and in he went.

This car was emptier than the previous ones. Half a dozen people filled the car, which was also very different in its design. There was about half the number of benches, and the space made by the lack of them was filled with tables. The benches themselves were upholstered, the curtains thick and deep red.

The passengers in the car, their attire much more refined too, regarded Jesse with aversion. One man's goose-like neck pulled back and his Adam's apple bobbed when he gulped. The plump woman next to him in a burgundy day suit, all puffy at the shoulders, fanned herself at an even faster rate as Jesse approached.

Jesse held up his hands in an effort to settle some nerves. "It's okay, folks, I'm not one of *them*." The last thing he needed was a scream. Rich folk were often quick to bleat when in trouble, was his understanding of them. "Just stay in your seats and I'll soon be out of your—" Jesse stopped when he spied someone familiar hiding beneath one of the varnished tables. "Well, I'll be . . ."

"Hi, Jesse," came the voice of a very sheepish-looking Henry Pye, his face having garnered fresh smudges since their last meeting. Jesse reached under the table and pulled him out from under it.

"What the hell are you doing here, Henry? I'd like to know how you managed to stretch a dollar into a first-class ticket?"

Henry proudly displayed the dollar. "I didn't. I snuck on while the controller wasn't looking. Thought I might pickpocket some rich folks in Spokane."

Jesse dropped to his haunches and took Henry at eye level. He needed the boy to understand. "Do you realize the trouble you're in right now?"

"Ain't in trouble. They ain't here to rob me. I'm just gonna keep outta their way until they git gone." The kid wasn't an idiot, at least. Jesse was grateful he had his head screwed on, but now he had his welfare to think about. The kid was treating it like a game of hide and seek. It brought back a flicker of Jesse and his brother in the woods, his mother calling them for dinner.

". . . Hey, answer me! I said, what are you doing here?" Henry said.

Jesse glanced up and down the car. All clear still. "I'm trying to stop these people. And that's why I need you to get back under that table, you hear me?"

"I could help you if you gimme another dollar."

"You stay under there 'til this all through and done and I'll give you two."

"You got yourself a deal." Henry spat in his hand and offered it to Jesse to shake.

Jesse just patted him on the head. "Go on, get under."

"But you ain't shook on it."

"You've got my word and that's enough," Jesse answered, starting to walk away. He pointed to the table. "Now, get back down under that table!"

Henry Pye huffed and rolled his eyes. *"Fine."*

∽

THE DOOR HANDLE had been broken. This one must have been locked. *Probably in case of robbers,* Jesse mused. Outside, the wind howled hard, but the din of the steam engine was louder. As the chimney continued to spew a thick plume of grey steam, the noise of the pistons along with the turning of the gearing and flywheels made for an awful racket. Jesse reckoned he could fire his gun and anybody on board would be hard-pressed to hear it.

The big 4-6-0 engine was an old but reliable beast. The big ten-wheeler locomotive had become popular across the growing United States in the past forty years, because of its ability to pull heavier loads while maintaining good stability at very high speeds. This iron horse was a powerful beast indeed, only it had fallen into the hands of criminals, and that was a dangerous thing. If he wasn't careful here, at the very least Jesse could get himself killed. At the very worst, he could cause a disaster.

Jesse climbed up the rungs of the ladder on the back of the tender, a huge tank that held the water tank and the coal bunker and made up most of the body of the locomotive. Tentatively, he crossed it, reaching the bunker perched on top of it just in front of the driver's cabin. Mounds of coal lay inside the bin and Jesse used it as cover as he peered over and into the driver's cabin. The back of another robber. Shirtless and covered with sweat, his muscular features slick from the heat and the steam. He still wore his holster, though.

Jesse weighed his options for sneaking up. Between walking along the coal and then the drop down into the cabin, a jostle from the train or the unfortunate luck of the robber turning around would spell a bad end for Jesse.

He needed another play.

Jesse turned back, walking along the water tank, feeling the pumping vibrations of the gears driving the wheels. He descended the ladder and as he turned, he saw a figure in front of him. Drawing his knife on a reflex he stopped when he recognized who it was.

"Jesus, Roxie, I could've killed you there. What are you doing here?"

"There's an awful ruckus going on in that luggage compartment, I don't think things are going well in there."

"Do you know if they've gotten into the safe yet?"

"No, they can't even get through the door to the compartment. I managed to get in and take a peek. Come on and I'll show you!" She grabbed his hand and started to lead him back through the cabin.

They passed by Henry, who poked his head out from under the table, and Jesse had an idea. Roxie had been able to get the drop on him, and he didn't want that happening again. He let go of Roxie's hand and held up a finger to her.

"Henry, I need your help," Jesse said, kneeling at the table. "I need you to keep watch for anyone coming, okay? If you see someone start to make a move down to us, you come on down and tell me." Jesse then raised a teacherly finger and then added, "But only if you can keep out of sight!"

"But you told me to stay under here."

"There's an extra dollar in it for you."

"What? No way." Henry blew a raspberry. "I'd have to be all quiet and sneaky, and then I'd have to run as well. That ain't worth an extra dollar."

Jesse sighed. "Fine. Two dollars."

"*Five*."

"Jesus Christ," Jesse said. "I'm starting to think you're in on the robbery, kid." Jesse frowned. "*Deal*." At that, he stood up and took off with Roxie.

"You sure you don't wanna shake this time?" Henry called after him.

Jesse certainly did not.

∼

BACK IN THE car where Jesse had first boarded the train, Irene's face had found an even paler shade; her eyes were even more sunken. He thought about trying to comfort her, but there were more pressing concerns. It wouldn't matter much anyway if they all ended up dead.

On the way, Roxie had pointed out the blood on the gangway, and Jesse told her about his encounter with Mateo. She seemed happy enough that she was now a little bit safer on the train. He reminded her not to let her guard down.

"There's still three killers on board this train. Keep your eyes open."

"Actually," Roxie had replied, "there's still four."

Jesse had guessed what she meant; he'd replaced Mateo with himself.

Outside of the door to the luggage car, they'd quieted down plenty. Jesse brought his blade to bear, while Roxie eased the door open. He could hear a strained voice, very agitated, and knew it belonged to Eddie Bradshaw. His best-laid plan wasn't unfolding as foretold, it seemed.

"Hey," Jesse whispered. "You don't have to do this."

"And sit in here and wait to die? No, thank you," Roxie replied and crawled into the luggage car. It was not the answer Jesse was hoping for. Now, if he got caught up in a fight, he'd have to keep tabs on Roxie and make sure no harm came to her. He hoped she wouldn't prove too much of a distraction as he followed closely behind her.

The luggage car stank. The damp in the corners and the dust in the air had mixed to create quite a musky odor. They were hiding behind one of the two shelves into which suitcases and duffels had been jammed, secured with ropes that were fraying in places. The odd bag had slipped through the restraints and now several were strewn across the dusty floor.

On the other side of the car, where the racks ended, was an open space. Phelps was propped up against the end of the rack. It didn't look like he was moving. Next to him, Mr. Wood was fiddling around in the big duffel bag, which was now on the floor. Eddie Bradshaw stood facing the far wall, guns holstered, hands on his hips, pushing back his khaki town coat. Jesse saw now that it wasn't in fact a wall, but a huge sliding door. Made of thick and sturdy wood, no doubt it was reinforced on the other side. A secure private compartment.

Inside of which was surely the spoils Eddie Bradshaw was seeking.

"Come on, Allen. I'll kill him," Eddie said now, raising his voice. Jesse could hear him loud and clear and noted the frustration in his normally cool and controlled cadence. "I'll kill your partner. Milton here isn't lookin' too hot either, my friend. So let's not draw this out any longer'n we need to, okay? Just open up and let us in. We'll do our thing and be done. No harm. No foul." Eddie hawked up a glob and spat it on the floor. "Shit, if you're worried you'll get in trouble for just opening up the damn door, we can make it look like we blew it up afterward. The safe, too." Eddie glanced behind him at Wood and Jesse ducked his head back a little, not wanting to be spotted. "My partner here is almost ready. You're running out of time, Allen. And I'm afraid my patience is runnin' a little thin, too. And you would *not* want to be around me once it runs dry. Trust me."

A threat. *So, the charm was a mask that was now starting to slip,* Jesse thought. He might be able to use that. Jesse made a mental note: don't give him time to think. It wasn't much, but he'd take any edge he could get at odds of three to one.

"No," came a weedy voice, muffled by the massive door. "I don't think so. I think I'll just stay behind here until we get to Spokane and help comes." That voice belonged to a kid. There was no way Allen on the other side of that door had seen enough birthdays to be doing that job. He had a pair on him though, standing his ground for somebody else's money.

Eddie took off his hat and fanned it at his face. "How many times I gotta say this to you, Allen?" he said. Jesse could almost hear the strain in his vocal cords as Bradshaw held back his exasperation. "My friend, this train is no longer on its way to Spokane. We are not going to meet your other Pinkerton friends. There is no backup. There is *no one* here or coming here to save you! Do you *understand* me? No one. Nobody. Not a single. Damn. Person."

"Y-yes, sir, I do," Allen stammered. "If it's all the same to you, I think I'd prefer to keep this door shut."

Eddie sighed heavily. He looked at the bigger man, Wood, who just shrugged and carried on fiddling in his bag. Jesse looked over at Roxie and she met his gaze with her big blue eyes and gave a twist of the head that said *well? Ain't you gonna do something here?* But what could he do? The gaps between the luggage stores were too narrow to get through, so there was no way of getting close. If he stepped out, that big guy Wood would spot him, and they'd fill him full of lead.

Jesse eyed the ropes holding the luggage, and he felt the beginnings of an idea sparking to life in his mind. A bad one, he soon realized, all he'd manage to do by cutting the ropes was make it a little harder for them to get back through the car.

He'd just have to wait a little and let things play out a bit longer and hope for an opportunity to arise.

That was when Phelps lifted his head with a groan. Eddie and Wood both snapped their attentions to him in unison. "A-Allen." He hacked a mightily unhealthy cough. "Allen . . . you hear me, kid?"

A pause. "Yes. Yessir, Mr. Phelps, sir."

Wood and Eddie continued to watch the old-timer. Jesse's eyes seemed to glow, either with fear, excitement, or anger, Jesse couldn't quite work out which. Maybe it was all three, anticipating what was about to come out of Phelps's mouth.

"Open the door, kid."

Eddie's face softened and that boyish grin appeared across his face.

"Just open the door. It ain't worth it. They got enough dynamite here to blow up the whole train. We lost this one."

Jesse swallowed hard. Wood was rummaging around in a bag full of *dynamite*? Eddie and his crew were not in the game of fooling around. And that bag may as well be another man with a gun. Dynamite was volatile, a woman with a fiery temper. You mishandle her and she was apt to blow and make you feel it.

Eddie turned his attention to the door. "Come on now, Allen. You heard your partner here."

From behind the door, there was a weighty *Thunk!* Another followed, then came several swift scratches, like metal gliding along metal. The door thumped again, then started to open inward.

"Stop!" Eddie said. Authoritative without raising his voice.

The door froze.

"I'm not going to be walking into the end of a scattergun or six-shooter, am I?" Eddie asked. He looked over at Phelps, still nursing his busted lip.

"Allen, hand it over."

Another pause. Then, the big door moved in slightly and the butt of a gun slowly poked through the gap. Eddie grabbed it and pulled it the rest of the way through.

Wood stood up and pushed the door forward and Jesse could see into the cramped compartment. A huge safe—at least six feet high– sat on the other side of that door. Dwarfed next to it, no more than five and a half feet tall, was Allen himself. His narrow frame looked gaunt and feeble next to the men striding in before him. His face was pockmarked with old acne scars, and it seemed his head hadn't quite caught up with the size of his nose just yet. Another couple of years of growth would sort that right out, Jesse hoped. For the kid's sake, at least.

"A fine weapon," Eddie said as he marveled at the twin-barreled shotgun in his hands. "And a fine choice you just made, Allen." Eddie waved the barrels in Allen's direction. The kid did his best to stand firm, but the shivers and the wet patch on his pants did little to sell the show of gallantry. "Now, you just need to make one more fine choice, and we'll trouble you no more. We'll be out of your hair and among the willows."

"What . . ." Allen started, his voice creaking. He cleared his throat and started again. "What do you want?"

"Well, gosh, Allen, I'd love to play a few rounds of poker," Eddie said flatly. Then he waved the shotgun and his tone harshened. "What do you *think*?" Eddie jabbed a finger at the huge safe. Allen gave a shaky nod and scuttled to the safe.

A massive gunmetal gray box of iron, marked with gold lettering that Jesse couldn't make out from the other end of the car. Jesse heard the rattling clicks as Allen twisted the dial to input the combination, before reaching for the long handle and jerking it down. The safe door popped open with a thud, Allen using both hands and gritting his teeth as it took pretty much all his strength to pull the door open.

"Holy shit," Eddie said softly.

"Is that real, boss?" Wood drawled.

"I think it is, Leon. Look at it. Look at all that *money*."

"You was right, boss. This job'll set us up for life!" Wood was almost giddy.

"That's right." Eddie turned his head toward Allen beside the safe, his eyes still watching the money. Finally, he wrestled his gaze away. "Thank you, Allen. Was that so hard?"

"No, I guess not. What happens now?"

"You get paid, Allen," Eddie said and flashed him a grin. Then he raised the shotgun.

BOOM!

At that close range it did an awful lot of damage to Allen, tearing up his face and chest into a bloody mess. Allen fell back and slumped against the wall, smearing it with blood and bits as he slid down it.

Eddie then turned around and raised the shotgun again. It boomed once more as the slug punched into Milton Phelps's gut. The old-timer let out a wheeze and then his head fell forward. He looked like he'd sat down and slipped off into a doze, if not for the pool of blood growing around him.

Jesse had to grit his teeth at the pain and the ringing in his ears. Such a report in such close confines only served to make the blast all the more deafening.

Leon Wood had his hands over his ears, wincing. Eddie was grimacing too. He dropped the shotgun onto the floor and dug his fingers into his ears. Then he gave his head a shake. "My apologies, Mr. Wood. I didn't quite think that one through, my friend."

"It's okay, boss," Wood replied. "We got so much money now, I can buy myself a new set o' ears!"

Eddie regarded his accomplice with a pained expression of contempt. Then gave him a condescending pat on the back.

"Lookit that guy," Wood said, pointing at the wet, grisly remains of Allen. "You turned him into stew!"

"Shit, Leon, what kinda stew are you eating?"

Wood just smiled at him.

"Whatever," Eddie said, his head shaking slowly. "We don't need the dynamite here no more, do we? So here's what we do next." Eddie lifted his watch from his pocket and checked it. "We're on schedule and should be coming up to the mountain soon. I'll take the sticks to Brett, so we can make sure we get a big enough bang." Eddie reached down into the bag now and pulled out some sacks. "You take these and start packing up that money. When you're done, meet me up at the first-class car. Understand?"

Wood nodded. "Yes, boss, sure do."

Eddie reached down, picked up the canvas bag, and slung it over one shoulder. "All right, you get to it now, we don't have long."

Leon was unmoving, smiling at Eddie.

"Move your ass, Leon! Clock's tickin'."

Leon, with his empty sacks, ducked back into the formerly secure compartment. Eddie grinned to himself and started to pace forward in long, determined strides.

Jesse and Roxie exchanged a glance. Jesse shook his head at her and then retreated to the wall of the car. This was not the time to make a move. Steeped in shadow, he crouched down and pressed himself to the luggage rack, making himself as small as he could. Roxie had done the same.

The footsteps got louder until Eddie, his khaki frock coat now speckled with blood, came into view at the doorway. Eddie stopped and Jesse held his breath. Readied his knife. Prepared to pounce. Why had Eddie stopped? Had he seen something? Jesse waited for the man to move. They were sitting ducks, a look to his left or right and this was all over. A bead of sweat ran down Jesse's left temple. His mouth ran dry.

Eddie let out a long whistle. "Ah, wait 'til Knowles sees this haul. We're goddamn rich!" Eddie said to himself then stepped out of the luggage car.

7

START EVENING THE ODDS

When the door closed behind Eddie, Jesse let out his breath and waited for his heart rate to settle.

He rolled back the past few minutes in his mind, trying to process them. As he did, he left his hiding place and peeked out from the rack to look at Wood, who was now grasping handfuls of dollars from the safe. He grabbed stack after stack; there had to be tens of thousands of dollars in there.

The dynamite made sense now. So did them not needing to rob the passengers. But the most chilling of all, and he kicked himself for not figuring it out sooner, why they weren't wearing masks or bandanas. They weren't making any effort to conceal their identities because they had no need to.

Everyone on this train was going to die.

Eddie's crew had ample dynamite for the safe, which they would now use elsewhere. The only place that made sense was the engine. They were going to blow that up and derail the train. But that was no guarantee to kill everyone on board. Rare it was, but there had been survivors of some pretty terrible derailments in recent years.

The mountain!

There wouldn't be any survivors if a train derailed off the side of a mountain. Jesse scratched at the stubble on his chin. He couldn't let these people die. And he couldn't let Bradshaw get away with the murders he'd already committed.

It was time to fight back.

And that started with Leon Wood.

Roxie had left her hiding place now and joined him in the middle of the car. Jesse kept his eyes on the man packing the bag with money. "Winona, I need you to stay here," he whispered.

"Who's Winona?"

He looked at her as he realized his mistake. "Sorry. She's . . ." Again that label he couldn't quite grasp. "A friend." It made him think about how much he missed her, but also how glad he was that she wasn't here.

"Well, I hope she's pretty if you're mixing her up with me."

"Stay here, okay?" Jesse said, holding up the palm of his hand this time.

"Okay, I'll stay here. What're you gonna do?"

"Start evening the odds."

Jesse watched Leon for another minute, studying the man kneeling in front of the big safe. Jesse observed as he took fistfuls of money and dumped them into the bag down by his side. His back was turned the whole time, his attention fully on the task at hand, with little appreciation for his surroundings. The man's lack of awareness was Jesse's advantage to exploit.

Jesse started forward, steadily and silently moving down the luggage car, grateful for the silence made by the lack of spurs on his boots. A long time ago he'd once opted not to have them for the sake of his horse, and soon noted the added stealthy benefit they provided and kept it as a rule whenever he got new ones.

As Jesse closed the distance, he pictured the fight ahead in his mind. Leon Wood was bigger than he was, no argument there, but he wasn't nearly as big as Slim Joe. Leon had about a foot on Jesse, but he was fat. Fat made a man slow, sluggish, and predictable in his movements. Jesse could outflank him if he kept on his toes and struck vulnerable parts. A good kick to a knee could shatter it, given enough force. A blow to the kidneys could slow him further. Or several well-placed nicks with a knife would bleed him eventually. But a big man like Leon would take time to bleed out.

Time Jesse didn't have.

This needed to be quick. Jesse held the knife, blade pointed down as he reached the end of the racks. To his right, Phelps sat peacefully in a pool of his own blood, which was now a much darker shade of red. Jesse would go for a killing blow once he got close enough, driving the knife deep into Leon's meaty neck until he felt bone.

Jesse reached the threshold of the secure compartment. His heart rate was drumming in his chest, his pulse pounding in his neck. His body was taut with nerves as he let out a long, silent breath. He needed to be calm and nimble. Not tense and rigid. He took a step forward and raised the knife, while Leon was still clawing at wads of cash and thrusting it into the bag.

Behind him, Phelps let out a wheezing moan. Jesse looked back as the old-timer finally slumped to the side and his cheek hit the thick pool of dark blood. Jesse looked back at Leon, who was now no longer stuffing money into the bag. Half his face a mottled mess of lumpy scarred flesh, Leon's face bore half a grimace as he regarded the intruding Jesse.

Oh, hell.

Jesse thrust forward, his plan of attack laid in ruins, as Leon started to rise. Jesse darted in with the knife and propelled it forward. Leon ducked into a roll and evaded it, with a speed that took Jesse by surprise. Maybe Leon wasn't so slow after all; this wasn't going to be as straightforward as he hoped.

As Leon got up, he freed his revolver and drew it on Jesse. Before he could properly aim it, Jesse lashed his knife in a wide rising arc to his right. The blade sliced across the knuckles on Leon's hand. The gun slipped from his fingers as blood rushed from a deep cut across his knuckles. Leon grasped his bleeding hand and tried to flex his fingers. Only the index responded. He then howled with an animalistic rage and barreled at Jesse. He ducked back into the luggage car as Leon bashed his fists into the wall, shaking free dust and splinters. Leon rounded on Jesse again, baring yellow, blocky teeth.

Jesse lamented the dropped revolver, out of reach in the secure compartment. Luckily it seemed that Leon was too blinded by rage to even think about reaching for it. If he did, Jesse wasn't sure he'd be able to close the distance quickly enough this time.

Jesse took a few swipes with his knife at the air, as he danced from one foot to the other. He was attempting to remind Leon of the damage he had done, and what he could do again. Jesse was also trying to buy himself some time to figure out his next move. He needed to bait Leon into exposing an artery. If he could just get one good swipe at the inside of a thigh or an armpit, it would be over.

Leon moved forward and Jesse danced back, not noticing Phelps's pool of blood had grown since his final slump. He put his foot down on the slick surface and it slid out from under him. His leg shot up and Jesse flew backward, crashing into the floor. Jesse rolled into the impact, seeing his momentum carry him over into a back roll and back on his feet.

As he looked up, Leon was charging at him, mere feet away. He glanced around him, noticing the fraying ropes holding back the overstuffed luggage. Jesse lashed his knife. The severed rope unleashed an avalanche of suitcases and trunks that bombarded Leon. He covered his lumpy face with his arms as the luggage pushed him into the other rack.

Leon was pinned beneath the weight of the luggage, his one free hand grasping at a case to ease his burden. Jesse darted forward with the knife, aiming to plunge it into his neck.

Leon's other hand burst through the luggage pile and struck him in his side. A white-hot pain bloomed in his ribs and Jesse cried out. Still badly bruised from his fight with Slim Joe a week earlier, that intense pain was born anew. Jesse stumbled, dropped the knife, and clutched his side as he staggered back and slumped to his knees. His vision rippled and his breath left him. He tried and tried to breathe in but his lungs wouldn't do as they were bid. Each choked gasp would only bring air as far as the back of his throat. Darkness pulled at the corners of his vision.

His swimming perception saw Leon push away the last few suitcases and a large trunk that he slid aside with alarming ease.

Jesse's lungs finally allowed in a breath of air, and he heaved in a few more. He started to get back to his feet when a hand grabbed him by the shoulder and slammed him into the luggage rack. He felt his Stetson fall away before he was pulled back and slammed into the other rack. Pain shot through his spine and joined the other shrieking alarms across his body.

Leon grabbed a handful of Jesse's shirt, turned, and launched him into the pile of suitcases. He crashed into them, the edge of a trunk scraping his head. Jesse pushed himself up. Grogginess clouded his mind like one too many whiskeys. He looked around as he heard approaching footsteps. Among the fallen luggage was the end of the rope he'd cut, dangling like a lifeline. He grabbed it, hoping to pull himself up. Instead, two meaty hands grasped his shoulders and yanked him to his feet. Jesse was spun around, and he stood there, swaying gently, fighting to stay upright.

"Yer that feller that was with the Pinkerton," Leon said, the penny having taken its time to drop. He chuckled and reached into his belt and pulled out a familiar-looking gun.

My gun.

"I'm gonna kill yer with yer own gun. That'd be real funny, I reckon." Jesse wasn't sure if it was the blow to his head or if the man really talked that slowly.

Jesse blinked rapidly, trying to will away the fog and bring back some clarity to his vision. He stumbled back and didn't fall, saved by the rope he'd forgotten he was holding onto. He leaned against the empty rack, letting the rope go slack. Jesse hoped Leon would keep talking a little while longer before he decided to kill him with his own gun so he could catch his breath.

"Hey," came Winona's voice from his right.

No. Roxie's voice.

Leon turned his attention to Roxie. "What the hell are *you* doin' in here?" He yelled at her.

Adrenaline surged through Jesse's veins, giving him that moment of clarity. His vision sharpened and so did his reflexes. He felt a sudden steadiness within himself and seized the opportunity to strike while Leon's head was turned.

Jesse pulled the rope up and looped it around Leon's neck once, and then again. He then grabbed the frayed end with both of his hands and dropped to the ground. The rope creaked as it tightened around Leon's neck under Jesse's full weight. Leon grunted and jerked forward but stayed on his feet, Jesse hanging a few inches off the floor. Leon's big hands reached for Jesse, trying to find purchase on his arms to no avail.

He crashed down on top of Jesse and again he felt the wind squeezed from his lungs by unseen hands. He couldn't let go. He *wouldn't*. Jesse twisted his forearm around the rope and pulled as hard as he could. He watched Leon's face turn scarlet, his eyes bloodshot and bulging. After what seemed like an age, that scarlet darkened into maroon and then a sickly shade of purple. Leon's legs bucked and his meaty fingers (the ones that still worked anyway) clawed weakly at him, and then more weakly still. Finally, Leon lay still on top of him.

Jesse held on for another few seconds to be sure, before finally releasing his grip on the rope and lying back, gasping for air, every inch of his body seemingly crying out in pain.

Another one down.

Roxie rushed over and helped Jesse heave the dead man off him, and then she eased him up into a sitting position.

"Goodness, Jesse, are you okay?"

"Yeah . . . never . . . better," Jesse said between wheezy breaths. "I just . . . need a . . . minute." Jesse sat a minute, appreciating the ability to breathe normally again (Well, almost. It felt like needles in his ribs with every breath) and that he still had all his fingers and toes. Despite the new bruises and the cut on his head, he was still good to fight and that was what mattered.

Roxie opened a suitcase and dug around in there, eventually coming out with a shirt. She tore it up and then knelt over Jesse, wiping up the blood that was torrenting from the gash on his head.

"Is it bad?"

"No, ain't too bad. Can't see your skull, at least. Head always bleeds plenty. Not sure why."

"Brain needs a lot of blood," Jesse said.

"How'd you know that."

"Doctor told me once. Not my first head injury."

"I'm sure. I'll bet it won't be your last, neither." Roxie tore off another strip and this time swept back Jesse's dark hair. She then wrapped it around the cut, tying it off into a crude bandanna. "There, that should do."

"Thank you."

He stood up, then waited for the bout of dizziness to settle itself down and reached for his Stetson. He was careful to place it back on his head without disturbing his bandage and aggravating the cut. Then he knelt over Leon Wood's body and picked up his Colt Single Action Army. "Hello, beautiful," Jesse said. "You miss me?" He then holstered it, and it felt good to have that weight on his hip again.

"Are you quite finished?" Roxie said as she handed him his knife.

"I am," Jesse said, sliding the blade back into his boot.

"So, what'll we do now?"

"Well," Jesse began as he adjusted his hat, "that's two down. Two to go. I'm gonna see if I can't better our odds any further."

"But why? Why don't we just leave?"

"You wanna jump off a train at this speed, be my guest. And besides, If I leave, that'll mean none of these other passengers will. And that is something that I just won't do."

8

EITHER WAY, IT'S OVER

Jesse pulled the gun from Leon's holster, wary of the dead man's bulbous, bloodshot eyes staring up as if to ask, "Killing me wasn't enough?" He thought about the blood on his hands again, and how it seemed like trouble just loved to follow him around. First Fortune, and now this, in the space of a week. He was tallying up quite the body count.

But they deserved it.

That's what he told himself as he felt the heft of the weapon. But it wasn't quite the case with Leon now, was it? Jesse had decided to kill him, and in cold blood, at that. Sure, he was party to a gang of thieves and killers and was most likely guilty of those very crimes himself. But didn't he deserve a chance to walk away? A chance that Jesse had denied him with his cowardly attack.

Jesse looked over at Roxie, her fiery hair framing a face painted brave. It made him think again. Leon had made his choice when he was happy to blow up a train full of innocent people. Anyone like that was beyond second chances. They were nothing but monsters dressed as men. Eddie Bradshaw and his other friend on this train would go the same way.

There was barely any room for fighting on this train, but from what Jesse had seen of these train robbers, there was even less room for talking. Poor Allen and Phelps had played along with them; look how they'd ended up.

This was self-defense for him and everybody on this train.

Jesse rolled the cylinder of the gun, satisfied that it was loaded. Then he spun it around and clutched it by the barrel, offering the grip to Roxie. "You know how to use one of these?"

"I know my way around a gun, sugar." She took the gun and spun it twice.

"Well, ain't you just a piece of pudding," Jesse said, and then he realized he was smiling. The past few hours had been rather grueling. It was about time he got himself a slice of luck. If Roxie was as good with her aim as she was handling that gun, his odds had just increased a fair wedge. "First things first: we need to do something about that money."

"Like what?"

"I'm thinking we need to take it off the board. We put it back in that safe and there's nobody else on here with the combination. Game over for them."

"What're you, *crazy*?" Roxie blurted.

Jesse's eyebrows met in the middle. "I miss somethin'?"

"You really think he's gonna be nice when he realizes he's got no money? You might be able to stop this train, but are you gonna be able to stop him when he just starts shootin'? Or throwin' dynamite in every car?"

Jesse looped his thumbs through his belt and considered. He felt the rhythmic thrum of the train over the rails and listened to the clacking of the wheels on the tracks. All the while, Roxie regarded him with desperate eyes.

"You're right."

Roxie sighed. "Thank you."

"No, thank *you*. It's nice to get a second opinion sometimes. Especially after two good beatings and a few blows to the head." Jesse stepped over Leon's body and walked over to Roxie. "Okay, we leave the money here. They've gotta come through us to get it anyway. All we gotta do is make our way to them, make sure we ain't seen, and then . . . well, I'll figure that out on the way."

"Unless they go over us."

Jesse laughed. "At this speed? Nobody's that stupid."

~

THEY LEFT the luggage car together with Jesse taking the lead, Single Action Army in hand. He kept it low and by his side. Shocked faces turned to him like a flock to their shepherd. Jesse smiled at them, tipped his hat, uttered reassurances. He got back a few smiles.

"What happened in there?" a man piped up.

"Bit of a fight. They're a man lighter now."

"But there were gunshots."

"That was them killing the security people," Roxie said. That got a few gasps Jesse could have done without.

"Thank you, Roxie," Jesse said, and then addressed the car. "Don't worry. Nobody go in the car behind me. Hell, everybody, just stay in your seats and you'll be okay."

"Why? What are you going to do?" the same man said.

"I'm gonna take back this train."

Jesse glanced down at Irene. She was staring out the window, tears streaming silently down her face. He sat down on the bench next to her and gently laid a hand on her shoulder. "You okay?" he asked.

"I didn't want this," she said. Her voice was shaky and quiet. "I should have just stayed at home. At least I'd still be alive."

"Hey. You are alive, and nothing's gonna change that, okay?"

"At least it won't hurt anymore," she said absently.

"*Hey.*" The words came out a lot harsher than he expected and she flinched in her seat, then looked at him with wide, somber eyes. Jesse knew that look, had seen eyes like that before. Eyes expecting a beating. It made his stomach twist. "I'm sorry, Irene." He moved his hand and she flinched away from it. "But listen to me, I'm going to get you off this train. And when I do, you're going to tell me exactly what it is you're running away from. You got that?"

She nodded gingerly. And Jesse took that as a cue to leave. No point in adding anything else to her discomfort now, was there? He got up from the bench and stepped back into the walkway.

~

JESSE WENT through the train cars with Roxie in tow. Still keeping his gun low, still giving those passengers that same, confident smile, and offering assurances that everything was going to be okay. The pair of them passed through two of the cars easily enough, but something wasn't quite right about the next one as they entered it.

"Were you in this car when you got on this train?" Jesse asked Roxie.

"Yeah."

"Something about it feel different to you?"

"Now that you mention it, yeah. There weren't this many people on it when I left it, that's for sure."

That was it. There were fewer occupied benches the last time Jesse was in here. This car had gained a few extra passengers.

"Somebody tell me what happened in here?" Jesse called out to the people in the car.

"Yes," a thin man with a monocle said. "That damned fool covered in blood forced us all out of the first-class cabin."

"And what of the boy?" Jesse asked.

The monocled man simply shrugged and said, "He's still in there."

That changes things, Jesse thought. He'd planned to go in and take the shot the moment it presented itself. There wouldn't be much in the way of cover; wooden benches weren't the best at stopping bullets. Slowed them down a bit maybe, but the lead was still going to punch a hole in him, too. A conversation wouldn't achieve much now either, would it? Jesse had seen the word of Bradshaw in action. The man spoke through both sides of his mouth.

But Eddie had Henry. That ruled out guns. At least until he could get Henry out of the crossfire.

Unless he was already dead.

Jesse shook away the thought and turned to Roxie. "Bradshaw and his pal will have a young kid in there. No more'n ten years old. Any ideas?"

"What about your idea?"

"I figured I'd go in there and shoot him."

"*That* was your plan?" Roxie said, looking at him wide-eyed.

Jesse shrugged. "You sound as surprised by it as I hope he'll be."

"Those blows to the head have done more damage than you realize, Jesse Clayton. You remember that *is* your name, right?"

"Yes. And you're Roxie . . ." Jesse scratched at his stubble as he thought to himself. "Can't quite recall your last name, though."

"Well, I wouldn't worry yourself there, sugar."

"How so?"

"'Cause I didn't give it." She winked.

"Oh, come on. We're wastin' time," Jesse said.

∼

THE GANGWAY LOOKED CLEAR, and the first-class car looked empty, so the two of them crossed as the wind howled around them like ravenous wolves. Finding cover on either side of the door, Jesse risked a peek inside. He saw Henry sitting at one of the tables, munching away at an apple, bubbling juice running down his chin. Across from him and sticking out of the upholstered seats, Jesse could see a pair of boots crossed over one another.

A scuffed pair of cavalry boots.

Oh, hell.

"It's bad?" Roxie asked.

"Is it that obvious?"

"Your face does kinda give it away, sugar."

"Henry's in there, all right. Sitting right across from Bradshaw, who's lying down. Could be sleeping. Could be waiting. Either way, there's nothing I can do to stop him from killing Henry, should he be of a mind to do it."

"Shoot him through the bench?"

"That's not a bad idea, Roxie. But I can't be sure it'd be a kill shot, or if I'd hit Henry. I'm not putting the boy at risk." Jesse paused, reassessing the situation. "There's only one way I reckon I can play this. I'm gonna walk in there, talk him outta that booth and into the walkway."

"Then what?"

"I'll draw on the son of a bitch."

∼

JESSE STEPPED into the first-class car, and still, it struck him how much better the quality of it differed from the others, right down to the flooring. He made a note that should he get through this, he'd inquire about a first-class ticket on his next trip.

Roxie followed him and closed the door behind her.

"Who's there?" Eddie called out from behind the seats.

Henry crunched his apple, his eyes widening with recognition. "Jesse!" he exclaimed, spurting spittle and chunks of apple onto the table.

"Jesse Clayton? Is that you?" Eddie called again.

"Certainly is. Got a friend with me, too." Jesse took a few more steps into the car, careful to give himself enough range on Bradshaw. He waved a hand behind for Roxie to stay back. He then moved his frock coat away from his hip and let his hand hover around the holster.

"Really? And who might your friend be?"

"Roxie," she called to him.

"Interesting. Now, I suppose that if you two are here with me, I would be correct in assuming that my associate, Mr. Wood, is no longer with us."

"You'd be right in thinkin' that, yes."

Bradshaw shot up from his prone position. Jesse's hand flickered toward his gun.

Not yet.

Bradshaw's friendly grin looked rather unsettling now that he was dappled with blood. It gave him more of an unhinged look. Maybe he was. He had no problem with killing folks, even when they were helping him. "What happened to him?"

"He got a little tied up," Jesse said flatly.

"Ah." Eddie nodded. "I saw a bit of blood out on one of the gangways. Would that belong to my other associate?"

"Marino?" Jesse deliberately said the wrong name.

"*Mateo.*" Eddie snapped his correction. The bait had worked. Get him unsettled, that's what he needed to do. He'd be apt to do something impulsive then, like leave the relative safety of being near a young boy.

"Right, sorry. Guess I didn't really catch his name, him being so weak and easy."

Jesse watched Eddie's face twist.

"I can tell by your appearance, that isn't true." Jesse could hear the undercurrent of irritation in Eddie's voice.

"Oh, this?" Jesse pointed at his bloodied face and his bandana, which poked out beneath the brim of his hat. "This wasn't Matthew, no way. This was your big man, Leon. He tossed me around a little bit before I finally put him down. Almost had me, I gotta say, too. But Manilo? He went down easier'n a whore on nickel night."

"You lie!" Eddie sneered.

"No, really. He danced around a little with his fancy knives and I just waited. All it took was a quick left hook and then I just heaved him over the side. He even managed to cut himself with his silly little push daggers as he went. Made an awful mess, all that blood." Jesse tapped a finger to his chin. "Though, wasn't quite as awful as hearing him scream. Like a girl it was."

Eddie smashed a hand into the table and shot upright. "His. Name. Was. MATEO!"

"Doesn't matter now though, does it? Whatever's left of him is rolling around the train wheels as we speak." Jesse circled a finger as he said it.

Eddie eyeballed Jesse; his cheekbones stood out almost as much as the vein pulsing in his neck. His shoulders eased and his rigid face softened into a smile. He even laughed. "You know, you're *good*." He pointed his finger at Jesse. "You are really, *really* good. I'm impressed. Pushing my buttons and getting me all *riled* up." Eddie clenched his fists and shook his hands in a playful effort to look mad. "It was working, too. I was so ready to just *step* away from my little friend Henry here . . . and draw down on you. Who knows, you might have even got me. I'm pretty fast, but then so are you, I imagine.

"But, I'm not that stupid, my friend. I'm real sorry about that. You think I could plan and pull off such a great heist without some serious firepower up here?" He prodded a finger at his temple. "I mean, *come on!* Have you *seen* the money in that safe? It takes a little more than a few guns and a bit of dynamite to pull this off."

"Doesn't matter. Either way, it's over. You're outnumbered."

Eddie laughed again. "Ah, Jesse, you're good, you're *good*. But you're not quite *that* good, are you?"

Jesse's eyes narrowed.

"You see, your friend, Roxie behind you . . . well, I hate to tell you this, but she's actually *my* friend, Roxie." As Eddie spoke, Jesse heard the clicking back of a hammer. He felt cool steel pressing into the base of his skull. "Isn't that right, Miss Knowles?"

9

A MAN WELL OVERDUE A FALL

Jesse couldn't help but laugh. How could he be so goddamned stupid? Right there beside him all along had been Bradshaw's fifth man. Well, woman, actually. Knowles wasn't their boss. Knowles was his partner.

He thought back. Right throughout the train journey there had been clues. The lipstick on Phelps's collar. She'd been working her way down the train to try and find the Pinkerton agent, and then she'd used that little trick to mark him for Eddie. What she'd said about there being four killers on the train still. Jesse had thought she had meant him. She'd been referring to herself.

What are you doing in here? Leon's words in their fight rang in his head. The way he'd said 'you.' That was recognition in his voice, not surprise.

Her hesitance to lock the money back up in the safe made sense now, too. At the time she had been pretty quick to be against the idea, before raising a good point about a potential Bradshaw with nothing left to lose. That was just an improvised lie to keep her in the money. Well, she was pretty damned good. No wonder Eddie had her on the team.

She'd been toying with him all this time, keeping tabs on him to make sure he didn't go too far into derailing things. . . but not standing in the way of him taking out Mateo and Leon. In fact, without her intervention, Leon would have surely killed Jesse. But why?

It didn't add up. And that bugged him.

"Not bad, Roxie. It ain't often I get hornswoggled," Jesse said.

"Oh, please, it wasn't hard playing the damsel with you. I could see you just itchin' to be the hero." She said that as she plucked his gun from his holster and tossed it onto a table. She then bent to his left and fished the knife out of his boot.

"Careful now, don't be getting too friendly," Jesse said as he rested both hands over his belt buckle, one on top of the other.

"You watch what you say now, Mr. Clayton," Eddie said. He sounded more formal and less friendly now as he stepped out into the walkway. He had an air of victory about him, like a hog at the trough when the eating was good. His back was a little straighter, and he wore a shit-eating grin that Jesse just wanted to smack right off his face.

Eddie Bradshaw was a man well overdue a fall. And Jesse would make sure he got what was coming to him.

Jesse felt the gun dig in just a little too deep between his shoulder blades and imagined the smile on Roxie's face as she ordered him forward. He did as he was bid. Eddie stepped aside as they approached, then gestured for Jesse to sit down at the table opposite Henry.

Eddie pulled Roxie in for a kiss. She stopped him, pointing out the blood he was covered in. While they discussed matters of hygiene, Jesse's hands, now under cover of the table, started their work. Gently so as not to raise suspicion, he eased the push dagger from where he'd tucked it and slowly slid it up and into the sleeve of his shirt. He then tucked the tip into the cuff to keep it secure.

Jesse leaned over the table toward the boy. "Did they hurt you, Henry?"

"No," he said casually, then took another bite out of his apple. "They gave me food and everything. This is my fourth apple." Jesse looked over at Eddie, still with that shit-eating grin. If anything, it had widened with Henry's comment. "It's fine anyway. They said that I can just jump off when they leave, and I'll be fine."

"And you believe that? Henry, this train is going awful fast."

Henry started "Well—"

"—And he'll be *fine,* as long as he rolls into it," Eddie finished for him. They were filling the kid full of food and lies. Of course, he'd believe them. He'd been raised on the street and never even been on a train. They could tell him it runs on sunshine and Henry would swallow it like that apple. "Anyway, Roxie, baby, could you do the honors? I'm getting pretty tired of Mr. Clayton here."

"Goodbye, sugar."

Jesse looked to Roxie just as the butt of the gun crashed into his temple.

∼

I know these woods. The thin trunks of the pines are all crammed together like they're tryin' to keep warm. Snow tops their branches like thick cream. I hear footsteps crunching in the snow and I bob down, squeezing myself into the smallest I can possibly be, careful not to scrape against any of the twigs or thorns in the bush.

He's coming.

He's coming to get me!

The footsteps crunch louder and louder. "Jesse! Jeeeesse! I'm gon' find you!" I know that voice.

A hand bursts into the bush! Pulls me out and into the snow!

"Got you!" It's my brother, Jonah. All tall, with his creaky voice. He's on his way to becomin' a man, see. Not like me, who's all small and weak. Well, that's what Poppa says anyways. He giggles and I do too, sunk up to my neck in the fluffy snow.

A whistle blares and we know what that means. Good timing, too; my stomach is rumblin' something fierce. That's what Jonah would say, so I say it too, now. Jonah reaches down a hand and I take it, grateful for the pull up. "Come on," he says. "I'll race you back to the house."

"No fair. You're bigger than me."

"I'll give you a head start."

But I don't move. I look at the pine tree and suddenly I ain't much hungry no more. The tree all covered in deep scratches and—

∾

JESSE OPENED his eyes to find himself still in the fine and accommodating first-class car. He was on the floor. Drums pounded in his skull so hard he felt like he could puke. He tried to move, but his wrists were bound to the leg of a bench, his ankles to another. He also noted the lack of a pull on his body from the train's movement.

They had stopped.

Jesse looked around. At the end of the car toward the engine, he saw who he assumed to be Brett. He was about Jesse's size, although his shoulders were a little broader, and he had a thick dagger of a beard hanging from his chin. He caught sight of Jesse, and he showed him a piano key smile. His olive and brown striped poncho was slung back as he tossed the dynamite bag onto a bench. That bag looked empty now.

That wasn't good.

The door behind him opened and Eddie walked in. He shook hands with Brett and pulled him in for a hug. "You got everything you need?" he asked.

"I do. Your friend is awake too, boss."

Eddie looked over at Jesse and his face brightened. He strode over and then dropped to his haunches. "You know, Jesse, I am glad that you're awake. Just in the nick of time before I make my leave."

"Where's Henry?" Jesse said.

"The little kid?" Eddie waved a dismissive hand. "He's fine. He's back in one of the cars with a tin of peaches. Shoulda seen the look on his face when he tried one. He didn't need to be here while we prepared the train. He can just enjoy his last moments with everybody else, as the train approaches its final destination."

"Eddie," Jesse said through gritted teeth.

"What?" Again with that shit-eating grin.

"I *will* find you."

"Sure, you will, my friend." Eddie patted his bruised ribs just a little too hard and Jesse's body locked up with pain. He didn't make a sound. He didn't want to give Eddie the satisfaction. Eddie stood and walked back over to his friend. Jesse waited for the burning in his side to ease, and then pressed his forearms together and smiled.

He felt the cold steel of the push dagger.

"What else have you got to do, Brett?"

"Light the fuse. That's it, boss."

"Excellent." Eddie clapped Brett on the shoulder. "Roxie and I will depart now with the money. You get this train moving again and you light it up when the time is right. Then you leave, too. Your horse is tied up to the gangway outside. You get gone and then you know where to meet us, yes?"

"The Traveler's Rest. I ain't forgot."

"Good man, and goodbye." Eddie extended his hand, and the two men shook. Eddie then left the car. A few seconds later, Brett left too. Jesse watched him clamber up the ladder of the tender and walk out of view.

This was his chance. Bound by the ropes, Jesse twisted his hands. There was plenty of give in them, which allowed him to rotate his hands to face away from each other around the bench leg. He eased up the cuff of his shirt and gave it a shake, then tilted his arm and the push dagger slid down into his waiting hand.

He felt the tug on his body as the train shunted into life and began to pull itself along the tracks again, slow and sluggish at first, as if rousing itself from slumber. Pretty quickly it started to gather speed.

Blade poking through his fingers, Jesse worked the dagger like a saw, steadily severing the fibers of the rope. The way it came apart reminded him of tearing a piece of chicken. His stomach growled. After a couple of minutes, he was through the rope. He threw it off and sat up, checking to see if Brett or Eddie had returned. The coast was clear, so he worked to free his ankles.

Out of his restraints, he stood up and looked out the window. A horse was running alongside, tethered to the railing on the gangway. He strained his eyes and saw two more in the distance, a trail of dust kicked up in their wake as they rode across the dirt, headed for a thicket of trees. Roxie and Eddie.

The Traveler's Rest. That's where they were headed. And once he'd stopped this train, Jesse would be right on their trail.

They were irrelevant for now, and so Jesse turned his attention to the train. He moved to the door that would lead to the engine and caught sight of something inside the bag.

A stick of dynamite. It was missing its fuse, probably why it had been left in the bag, but Jesse knew enough about the explosive to understand it was still useful . . . if you had good aim. He left the dynamite in the bag alone and moved on, opening the door and stepping out onto the gangway.

The engine was plenty loud and that suited Jesse just fine. Brett wouldn't hear him. To Jesse's right was the horse, galloping alongside the tender, its reins tied through the railing. Honey colored with patches of white, the poor thing didn't have much choice in the matter. Jesse wondered just how much longer the mare could keep it up.

The black metal of the rungs was warm in his hands, having baked under the late afternoon sun. When he reached the top, Jesse knew the horse wouldn't have to run much longer, no matter what. In the distance, no more than a few miles of yellowing prairie between it and the train, stood a mountain. Wide, gray, and looming. The tracks snaked up and along its side. That was where Brett was going to blow the train, causing the cars to fall hundreds of feet down.

Jesse had a matter of minutes and needed to make every one count.

He kept low as he advanced along the tender. He might be hard to hear but he'd still be easy to spot. When Jesse reached the small square opening of the coal bunker, he froze. In among the black chunks of coal were rods of dynamite. At least a dozen of them, sticking out of the coal mound like birthday candles—the deadliest birthday cake Jesse had ever seen. Each stick had a cord protruding from it, all converging on each other to a point where they had been twisted into one. That line trailed off toward the driver's cabin.

Jesse lay down on the warm black metal. He leaned over the opening and reached for his push dagger. He was careful as he reached out for the cord: any jostling could set the dynamite off, temperamental mistress that it was. Jesse took hold of the fuse and brought the blade to it.

Movement in the corner of his eye.

Jesse dropped the cord and rolled to his side as Brett's boot swung through the space Jesse had just occupied.

The engine being loud worked both ways.

Jesse sprang to his feet and brought up the push dagger, standing side-on to Brett in a defensive stance. Brett just laughed, a grim display of missing teeth and donkey-like hawing. Tucked into his belt was Jesse's Colt. The thought crossed his mind that he'd need to give his gun a good clean after this was all through; she'd been in one too many unsavory places.

Brett's hand went for his gun and Jesse only had one choice. He leaped at Brett and the train robber stepped aside. Jesse scrambled to regain his balance, so as to not fall over the side and hit the ground at over forty miles per hour.

Brett ran across the tender and then jumped the gap between that and the roof of the first-class car. Jesse couldn't let Brett get range on him, or it would be all over. Despite the pain in his side, Jesse sprinted across the black metal. He jumped the gap easily and used the momentum to keep on running. He chased down Brett, who ran ahead, one hand clutching his hat that the passing wind and steam tried to pull away.

Jesse closed the distance and rammed his shoulder into Brett's midriff. Brett groaned as he hit the roof with Jesse on top of him, but he was not overcome. He struck Jesse on the chin, knocking him back. The wind plucked Jesse's Stetson from his head. Not that he noticed; he was too busy taking another two licks from Brett.

He didn't have the strength for another fight. His ribs burned with fury, his head was pounding, and he could feel the warm dribble of fresh blood down the side of his head. His fingers, the ones dislocated last week, were singing a song of pain all their own. Jesse needed to breathe.

Seeing Jesse defend his face with his arms, Brett grabbed the back of Jesse's coat and used it as a brace as he propelled his knee into Jesse's abdomen. What little breath remained now left him, and Jesse meekly put his hands on Brett's belt as he tried to stay upright.

Brett booted him over the side of the car.

Jesse wasn't quite sure how it happened. Maybe he knew of it from when he had been inside the car earlier; perhaps it was just the blind and desperate instincts of a man facing certain death; possibly even divine intervention. Before the hands of gravity could claim him, Jesse let go of the dagger, reached out, and found purchase on an open window. Several joints crackled as his body jerked to a halt and he clattered the side of the car.

A bolt of hot pain shot through Jesse's collarbone right up to his fingers. He dangled for a moment as his legs desperately poked the air for purchase, twirling back inward to the side of the train. Eventually, his boots found a footing on the protruding lip at the bottom of the car, and he was able to steady himself.

"Goddamn!" Brett shouted. The wind was trying to take his words like they had Jesse's hat. "You're a tough sumbitch, I'll give you that! Not surprised you kilt them two fools. But you ain't bestin' me. It's the end of the line for you now." Brett went to reach for his belt and then looked down all confused.

"Lookin' for this?" Jesse said as he swung up his free hand, pulling back the hammer on his Colt. He'd swiped his gun back when Brett had kneed him. The train robber's eyes widened in recognition. His hand flickered toward his holster.

The bullet struck him in the chin and Brett jerked up straight. He rocked one way and then the other, before falling forward off the train and into the ground with a crunch. Jesse watched his body roll once, twice, before coming to a stop among the gravel and dust.

Jesse holstered his gun and then shimmied his way across the side of the train, using what little strength he still had to stop himself from being pulled away by the hands of the wind tearing by. Jesse reached for the railing, clambered over it, and fell into the gangway. He just lay there, taking long, deep, and grateful breaths.

Then he remembered the mountain.

10

A COUPLE MORE FOR GOOD MEASURE

Despite what felt like his whole body protesting, Jesse forced himself up off the gangway. Almost home and dry. All he needed to do was cut that cord and the immediate danger was over. He had to brace himself against anything he could get his hands on as he moved through first-class: the door jamb, the benches.

"You need help there, Jesse?" came the voice of young Henry Pye. He wasn't ashamed to say he was glad to hear it. Jesse paused in front of the door and looked up at the tender.

"Yeah. Come with me," Jesse said and opened the door. He pointed at the ladder, and Henry climbed up, Jesse following.

"Hey, is that rope supposed to be all sparking and stuff?" Henry said as Jesse reached the top. His head darted up to see the fuse cord sparking just like Henry had said. The sparks ran across the cord and into the opening of the coal bunker.

Oh, hell.

"Henry, get down here now!" Jesse said and dropped onto the gangway. Pain be damned, he burst into the first-class cabin and went to the open bag. He dug through it with his hands, finding two sticks of dynamite. He only needed one. He dropped the extra back in the bag and limped across the car as fast as he could, Henry in tow.

Jesse shouldered the door open and crossed the gangway. He barged open the other door and said, "Everybody! I need you to move into the next car, now!"

Nobody moved, only stared at him blankly. The man with the monocle began to raise his hand.

"NOW, DAMMIT! MOVE!" People started scrambling out of their benches and rushed for the door toward the third car. *Good*, Jesse thought: he didn't need to wave his gun at them.

Jesse stepped out into the gangway, right where the plates separated over the car coupling. There was a slight gap where the two halves of the steel gangway met, jostling lazily with the movement of the train. Jesse knelt and could see the coupling mechanism underneath. Like two steel fists closed around a bolt thicker than his arm.

"Henry, go untie the horse and wait by it, okay?" Jesse said. Henry ran without a word. Jesse reached down and carefully wedged the dynamite between the gangway plates above the coupling. Satisfied it was in place, he took several limping steps back into the first-class car. He took a couple more for good measure. He then raised his Colt and fired.

BOOM!

The explosion shook the whole train, the car rattling so violently on the tracks that Jesse almost lost his footing. When the smoke cleared, he moved as quickly as he could back to the scene of the detonation. The steel of the gangway was all distorted out of shape, revealing the coupling all battered and bent too. Steel whined as it ground together now. But the coupling remained intact.

Oh, hell.

Hearing an almighty whine of steel shrieking, Jesse looked down to see the coupling crack and then break apart. The locking pin and loose pieces fell under the train, making terrible clanging noises as they got caught up in the wheels and the track.

Jesse felt a sense of relief as the car started to pull away from the rest of them, leaving them to come to an idle stop safely on the prairie. He'd done it. He imagined the whoops and cheers onboard those other cars now.

Nobody else was dying today.

"Jesse! Jesse!" Henry called to him, and he turned to see the boy distraught, tears threatening the corners of his bloodshot eyes. His hands were empty.

"Henry, where's the horse?"

"It . . . the horse when the bang . . . it scared me and . . ."

They surely had no more than a minute now. He'd used up so much time separating the cars, they had nothing left. Outside, the prairie was gone. On one side was the gray wall of the mountain rock, on the other, blue sky. Jesse looked around for something, anything to use as a means to get off this train alive. He hadn't come this far to die now.

"Henry, listen to me. I need you to start grabbing as many of the curtains as you can. Just pull them off their railings, you got it?"

The boy nodded and the two of them started pulling at the soft green curtains. Every one that Jesse pulled down he tossed to the other side of the train. He wasn't sure it would work. But if they could wrap themselves in enough layers, it might just save their skin when they hit the ground. All he had to do was—

He felt it in his bones first. The deep rumbling ran right from his metatarsals up to his teeth. He felt a sensation of flying, an unseen hand at his back, pushing him up and into the cei—

11

THE BLOODY WAY OF DOING THINGS

A whistle blares and we know what that means. Good timing, too. My stomach is rumblin' something fierce. That's what Jonah would say, so I say it too, now. Jonah reaches down a hand and I take it, grateful for the pull-up. "Come on," he says. "I'll race you back to the house."

"No fair. You're bigger than me."

"I'll give you a head start."

But I don't move. I look at the pine tree and suddenly I ain't much hungry no more. The tree is all covered in scratches and my brother says that bears do the scratches to sharpen their claws or nails or whatever it is they call 'em. So they're even better at eatin' people. I ain't never seen a bear and don't plan to.

Jonah tells me to come on and pulls me by the arm. He drags me back to the house and I open the door and there's Momma. She's all blurry but I know that she's beautiful. I can't hear what she's saying but it makes me smile anyways.

I'm sitting at the dinner table with Momma and Jonah now, a big pot in the middle of the table all steaming and smelling good. Momma nods at me to open it up and I do. I look inside and there's nothing there but a crumpled sheet of paper. I know that sheet of paper. I look back at Momma and she gives me an encouraging nod. She's still blurry but somehow, I know she's smiling.

I reach in and pick up the creased paper. I go to unfold it, and I know what it's gonna say.

The door bursts open. I see a silhouette I know pretty well. Poppa was back. I shrink down back into my seat, and I look at Jonah and Momma, but they're gone now. I look back at Poppa and he's gone too. It's just me alone in the house on my chair now. Still holding my piece of paper. I open it up and I expect to see a name. Instead, I just see one word.

GO.

∽

JESSE WOKE WITH A GASP. He was lying on the floor of the train car, but something felt *off*. He heard the low whine of metal bending in a way it shouldn't. He pushed himself up onto his elbows and saw what was wrong.

The front end of the train car was gone.

There was nothing left but warped and torn steel. It fell away to a sheer drop. The car was hanging over the edge of the mesa. A few hundred feet below were trees and a river. And what remained of the locomotive.

Jesse grabbed for the nearest bench and pulled himself to it. The act caused the car to groan and shift slightly. He stayed perfectly still as the car creaked and slowly settled down again. Once it was still, he looked around for Henry. Jesse saw broken and loose benches, curtain rails hanging, and shattered windows. But no Henry.

"Henry?" Jesse called out. "Henry!" He said again, not daring to shout in case it disturbed the train. He was fairly sure it wouldn't, but he'd taken enough risks for one day.

"I'm here," Henry replied meekly and from way down the car. "Help. *Please.*"

Jesse tentatively stepped along the walkway, reaching from bench to bench for support. He froze with every creak from the metal until finally, he reached the torn end of the car. A brisk wind rolled across him, and Jesse felt a chill. He looked down to see Henry clutching a curtain as he dangled over the precipice. White as a sheet. Teeth chattering in the cold. The green fabric was tearing, the rail all bent and sagging. Jesse realized that telling Henry to grab curtains had probably saved his life. Now he had to do it again.

Jesse lay face down on the floor. He braced a leg against a bench, held on to another with his hand, and then eased himself out and down, reaching an arm out to Henry. "Grab on to me, Henry. I've got you."

"No. nope. Ican'tdothatnoway." The kid's words came out all in a blur.

"Trust me, kid. All you have to do is just reach out one hand. I'll grab it and I'll pull you up. I promise," Jesse said. The car groaned as it shunted down. Rocks and grit went tumbling over the edge. There wasn't time for this. This train car was going to drop any second. "Come on. We don't have time, Henry. Just grab my hand. I'll lift you up and then we run like hell off this train. Okay?"

"No."

Jesse watched the curtain threads pull apart some more. Another moan from the broken train.

"Time's up, kid. I'm gonna count to three and then you're gonna gimme your hand."

"No."

"Wasn't asking. *One.*"

Curtain fibers peeled away from each other. A groan from the train.

"*Two.*"

The groan grew louder. Jesse felt the train shifting slightly. More rocks and grit fell from the edge.

"*Three.*"

Henry's hand shot out and the curtain gave way. Jesse clamped his hand to the boy's wrist and yanked with all his strength, swinging him up and back into the car.

"Run!" Jesse yelled and got up himself. As they ran forward, the train car was beginning to shift back. The train slid farther and faster to the edge of oblivion. They kept running. Faster and faster he ran, but Jesse felt like everything was moving but him. The train car started to tilt back now, too.

Henry jumped out first. Jesse was just behind him. The angle was working against him now, the hands of gravity getting stronger with each passing second forcing his legs to pump harder. He reached the doorway and realized there was nothing but air to step onto.

Jesse jumped, hanging in the air for seconds that felt like hours.

He hit the stones and scrambled for purchase as his legs dangled over the edge. Henry ran over and lent a hand as he pulled himself up. He stood up and let out a long breath. A moment later, they heard the distant crash as the train car hit the ground below. The two of them turned to watch the steel beast tumble and smash across the base of the mountain before rolling into the trees, felling two before finally settling to rest. Jesse looked down at Henry, who looked pale and shaken. The poor kid wasn't going to be sleeping right for a while, Jesse thought.

"You know what, Henry?" Jesse said as he looked back at the wreckage below them. "I've decided that I don't much like trains."

"I don't like 'em, either."

～

EDGING TOWARD THE HORIZON, the early evening sun burned a deep orange as it beat down on them. Sweat ran down his cheeks and he could feel it patching his armpits. Jesse didn't mind. This was the kind of sweat he could bear. It was much better than the *other* kind.

They'd been walking a fair stretch but still couldn't see the rest of the train yet. They'd reached the prairie again, having kept well away from the edge on their way back down the mountain. Jesse figured they had covered at least two miles, give or take a step.

For the first mile, they'd not said much to each other. Jesse glanced at the kid from time to time and wondered if he was just trying to process what he'd just been through. Jesse could barely think due to a ringing in his ears that he couldn't shake, a result of either the guns, the dynamite, or the deafening din of the steam engine.

Hell, it was probably all three.

Jesse had also taken the time to assess his injuries. He hadn't dared try to remove the improvised bandage on his head. The blood on it was almost dry and he hoped that was a good sign. His fingers were sore as hell. With every step, needles were jabbed into his ribs; the same went for his shoulder if he raised it more than an inch. The hefty slice on his forearm wasn't bleeding anymore either. He had a few aches and pains, but luckily, he hadn't suffered anything serious in the explosion. Come to think of it, both he and Henry had been might fortunate. He'd had worse and endured; he'd survive this too. Come winter he'd have a stiff joint or two, but at least he'd be breathing.

He was still limping, though.

"Hey, is that it?" Henry said, pointing at a vague box shape in the distance.

"Gotta be. No more than a few miles away. Won't be long until we can sit it out in the shade and wait for rescue."

"But what if they can't find us?"

"They will. Once they realize the train isn't where it's supposed to be, which they probably already have done, it won't be hard to figure out that somebody switched out the tracks. Ain't the first time something like this has happened. Won't be the last either."

"They'll take us back?"

"I hardly think they'll leave a few dozen people out here." Jesse glanced at the kid and saw his head hung low, watching the dirt he was stepping over. "Why'd you get on that train, Henry?"

The kid shrugged.

"Better yet . . . who are you?"

The kid looked up at him, top lip turned up in irritation. "I'm Henry."

"I mean who *are* you, Henry Pye?"

"What kind of question is that?" The irritation had trickled into his tone now.

"As in, what kind of person are you? Running around, stealing from folks, and jumping on trains to anywhere for no reason other than you could? That strikes me as a kid who doesn't know the answer."

"I know who I am. I'm just a guttersnipe. That's all."

"That's not what I mean, Henry."

"Then what? I ain't no mind reader."

"Who you are . . . is the choices that you make. And those choices always boil down to that one simple question: who am I? It's the question I live by. Am I the man who sits there while a train gets robbed, or am I the guy stupid enough to try and stop it? Am I the man that wants to do something or just keep on living?" Another question popped into Jesse's head: *Am I the guy who wants to be with Winona?*

"I don't get your point, Jesse."

"My point is, you ain't no guttersnipe. You're just *acting* like one."

"I'm doing what I'm doing to survive. Ain't nobody lookin' out for me but *me*." He jabbed a thumb into his chest to really ram home the point. Jesse thought he may have even puffed his chest out a little, too. This kid had just survived a robbery and a train crash. In Jesse's book, he'd earned the right to act the big hog now.

That meant talking to him like one, too. So Jesse did: "I've been right where you are, kid. Me and my brother once upon a time. No parents or anybody to look out for us. You remind me a lot of myself back then. True, we had each other, but I . . . well, let's just say I made some very questionable choices."

"You . . ." Henry started, then bit his lip, hesitating. ". . . did bad stuff, too?" The guilt in Henry's voice felt like another needle in his ribs.

"I did. And kept doing bad stuff . . . until it got *real* bad."

"But you're okay *now*."

"Not because of me. A woman I once knew who got me out of that life. At the cost of her own. Not long after . . . I guess I got lucky when a good man took me in. Him and me had a similar conversation. So I guess . . . I'm trying to do for you what he did for me, Henry. I ain't your daddy, ain't trying to be, but I know there's good in you. Hell, what you did up on that train to help me, while all those grown-ass adults sat there waitin' to die? You ain't a guttersnipe, kid. You're a damn hero to me. You just need a chance."

They were almost at the train now. The door of it opened and Jesse could make out a womanly shape waving at them. He was pretty sure it was Irene.

"A chance to do what?"

"To ask yourself who you are. We got a long wait ahead of us. We get in that car, you have a nap and think about it. When we get back to Rathdrum, if you know who you are, I'll help you the best I can."

Henry looked up at Jesse and gave him a shaky nod.

They reached the train, and two men disembarked to help the pair of them clamber into the car. When they did, the passengers erupted into a round of applause. Among them was Irene, who clapped and smiled at them, tears in her eyes.

And that bruise was still on her face. Another talk he had to have.

∼

JESSE COLLAPSED ONTO THE BENCH, as did Henry a few rows down.

Jesse shifted around on the hardwood, struggling to find a comfortable position. Eventually, he settled by swinging up his legs and resting his head on the window. At that moment he really missed his Stetson. That would have been perfect, tilted down to cover his eyes from that sunshine.

Irene kneeled on the bench in front and leaned over to inspect Jesse's face.

"What are you doing?" Jesse asked.

"Checking you're not badly hurt. That's a lot of blood," Irene said curtly. Her demeanor was much more assured than the last time he had seen her.

"I'm fine, really. But you can tell me how you got that bruise, now." Jesse regretted his words the moment he saw her shrink back, the confidence shattered with a sentence. He felt bad, but his pain was worse. He was suffering and therefore so would his patience, it seemed. "Come on, Irene. I'm back. Now tell me. Who is it that you're clearly running away from? Husband?"

She nodded slowly.

"And he's the one who went and re-colored your face?"

She nodded again. "It was a lot worse before. Worst it's ever been. I . . ." She'd started now, Jesse gave her the time to get really going, "I'd not worn the right dress. He said if I wanted to dress like a whore, well, he'd . . . he'd just go right ahead and treat me like one. I saw my face the next day and promised myself I'd leave as soon as I could see out of both eyes again."

"Brave of you."

"But it's not so bad now. And after something like this, well, maybe I—"

Jesse swung his legs around and leaned forward. "Now let me stop you right there, Irene."

"But with all that's happened maybe . . . maybe he'll change."

"And maybe he will, Irene. But what if he changes *back*?" That question lingered in Jesse's mind, as it was often one he posed to himself. The draw was always there, the pull to do things easy and profitable. The bloody way of doing things.

"Then I'd leave again."

Jesse shook his head. "Only way that man will let you slip through his fingers a second time is in the back of a corpse wagon, Irene."

A shadow fell across her face.

"What's your husband's name?"

"Clarence," she said, head bowed still.

"Will he be in Rathdrum when we get back?"

"Most likely. If not by now, he will in the morning."

"Well, if you'd like, maybe Clarence and I can have a conversation before you leave. And that's *if* you want to leave."

"Okay, Jesse. Thank you."

Jesse reached over the bench and gave her hand a reassuring squeeze along with a smile. Still with his hand in hers, he put his legs back up on the bench and leaned his head back on the window. "Wake me when help comes," Jesse said and closed his eyes.

Sleep came awful quick to him.

∼

"Jesse, wake up!"

His eyes opened and, in the blur, somebody was standing over him, shaking him.

"All right, all right, I'm up. What is it?"

"Riders."

Riders? Hell, that couldn't be good.

That could mean any number of things. Sure, it could mean help was coming. But it could also mean help *wasn't* coming. They could be bandits who had found themselves rather fortunate, which would be rather unfortunate for the people on the train. Or it could be Bradshaw and his friends, come to check on their handiwork and tie up some loose ends.

Jesse got to his feet. He crossed the car and looked out of the window, along with most of the passengers. Crossing the prairie in a line were five riders on horseback. A big plume of dust rose in their wake and from this distance, it was hard to make out any details as to who they were.

All they could do now was wait.

"How long's it been?" Jesse asked.

"A little over three hours," Irene said.

Three hours. Plenty of sleep. He had some stiffness, but his headache had eased and so had his shoulder. Imagine what a bed and a whole night's worth could do. Jesse pulled out his gun and inspected the chamber. He reloaded and then moved to the end of the car. "Everybody sit tight in here, okay? If they ain't friendly, I'll . . ." He thought about the five-to-one odds, and what he'd already managed to scrape through today. Surely his luck had run dry at this point. "I'll do what I can."

Jesse stepped out and then dropped onto the track. He rounded the car so as to have some cover from the approaching riders.

A few minutes later they were upon him. They split off, three riding to meet him, the other two splitting off to the other side of the train. They must have seen him get off and made a move to pincer him. Clever. These people weren't fools. They were professionals.

The sound of hooves beating the ground stopped.

"Now listen here, whoever y'are," came a voice from one of them. Jesse kept behind the train while it still provided cover. The voice had an authoritative, gritty maturity to it. It didn't sound outlaw, that was for sure. "You drop your gun and step out nice and slow like. You do that and things'll be resolved peaceful."

"And who might I be talkin' to?" Jesse called out, being careful to raise his voice without sounding threatening. He kept his gun raised and his body pressed to the train. He could feel the adrenaline building in him. Just waiting for that moment.

"Ephraim LeFleur, of the United States Marshal Service. You one of the men who sought to rob this train?"

"No."

"Then step out with your hands up."

Jesse holstered his gun. He didn't have much choice. The man sounded confident like he had a voice a man could trust, but then so did Jesse when he was pulling the long bow on folks. He raised his hands and walked out into the burning orange hue, the three riders steeped in shadow before him. A moment passed and he wasn't riddled with holes. As did another and he remained unharmed.

"That's far enough, friend," LeFleur said casually but it was an order.

Jesse did as he was bid.

"What's your name, then?"

Jesse went to speak his name, but he didn't get the chance.

"Hold on there a minute," said one of the other riders, the voice was female and very familiar. Still, it was hard to place, them still being in front of the sun. "*Jesse Clayton*, is that *you*?"

12

KNOWING WHAT YOU DON'T WANNA BE

That voice belonged to Sarah Grahame. She hopped off her horse and within a few strides of her long legs in those tight jeans, Jesse saw her fully. Her washed-out, tawny hair was pulled back tight in a serious ponytail, while her cheekbones were about as sharp as her tone. She had in her hands a Winchester, which was unceremoniously pointed in Jesse's general direction.

Feeling a jollying sense of relief, Jesse put his hands on his hips and smiled. "Well, you're a sight for sore eyes, Sarah. How long's it been?"

"Almost three years and twenty dollars." That rifle twitched a little closer. "You'd better be robbin' this train to pay me back." She had a husky voice that she liked to make worse with her cigarettes.

"I ain't robbed this train. There's a fair few people on board who'll back me up on that. I can pay you your twenty dollars too."

"Sarah, ease up now," Ephraim said. Underneath his white slouch hat was a tanned face lined so deep they could have been ridges. Bags sagged under his eyes, as did the skin around his jawline. The man looked old. But he was taller than Jesse, and while his gray duster hid much of him as it flapped in the breeze, it ran tight along his wide shoulders.

Jesse heard the door of the train car open and LeFleur's hand whipped to his hip and snapped back up with his Colt in hand. Age wasn't slowing him down any.

The man with the monocle was poking his head slightly through the gap in the door. "Is it safe?" he asked.

"Depends. This man here in front of me trying to rob you?"

The man looked horrified. "Sir, if it weren't for that man, I fear we'd all be *dead*."

LeFLeur looked back at Jesse, who couldn't help but show off a shit-eating grin of his own.

"Well, all right then," LeFleur said. He turned to the other rider. "Marsden. Ride back and give them the go-ahead. Let's get these people back to Rathdrum."

At that, Marsden pulled on the reins of his horse. It spun around and took off, galloping along the track.

It wasn't long before things got moving. A second engine, this one not quite as impressive as the 4-6-0 but hefty enough, towed the stranded train back to Rathdrum. Over the course of the journey, LeFleur was on board while his deputies had ridden ahead of them. He interviewed passengers, all telling the same story. He then sat down with Jesse, who outlined his role in the whole affair. The murdered Pinkertons, his killing of three of the gang, their names, and how Roxie had helped him at first before fleeing with the money along with Bradshaw.

Like any tale worth telling, it took time. Jesse was still talking as the train arrived at Rathdrum station. Everybody filed off and Jesse kept talking. Eventually, Jesse and LeFleur got off. It was much cooler now. Dusk had stolen away the sunshine and thrown darkness over the town. Gaslights cast everything in a greasy yellow glow.

"Any idea where they might have gone?" LeFleur asked.

"Bradshaw did have a conversation with his man, Brett, I think it was, shortly before he left. Mentioned a place called the Traveler's Rest. Sound familiar?"

LeFleur shook his head and put a quirley in his mouth. He struck a match on the sole of his boot and brought it to the crude roll-up. Jesse watched as the strands of tobacco curled up and shrank under the flame. "I'll ask around. Put a few feelers out. Someone around here will know, most likely." LeFleur blew smoke from his nostrils. "In the meantime, you get yourself some rest. When we do find them, you're coming along."

"Good. Thank you, Marshal."

LeFleur tipped his hat and went back to the train. Jesse walked on, joining the trail of passengers. He wasn't with them long before he was hooked out by the arm.

"I found this on the ride back here," Sarah said. She was holding a dusty Stetson hat. "You seem to be the only one here without a hat."

"I thought that was gone for good."

"It will be if you don't pay me my twenty."

Jesse pulled his money from his pocket and handed Sarah what she was owed. She popped the hat back on Jesse's head in return. "Now, if you'll excuse me, as lovely as it is to see you, Sarah, right now I'd just like to get some sleep."

"And here I was about to offer you a drink to catch up." Her little button nose wrinkled. "But you should probably get a bath before you sleep, Jesse. You're ripe."

"The best of friends are always those who are most honest."

"There's a room for you at the hotel just up ahead, by the way. I set it up with your lady friend, Irene. Room number four, up the stairs and opposite hers. Said to tell you the boy's with her too."

"Thank you, Sarah," Jesse said and waved goodbye.

Jesse entered the hotel. The man who greeted him did his best to hide his revulsion at the apparent reprobate that had stumbled into his establishment. He greeted Jesse, maintaining a polite tone. When Jesse said he was looking for room four, the man relaxed.

"You're Mr. Clayton?" the proprietor said in a nasal, curt voice.

"I am."

"Your room is upstairs. But before you retire to bed, Miss Berg has arranged for you to use the bathhouse. This way, please." The proprietor stepped from his counter and proceeded to lead Jesse down the corridor. His limbs were starting to feel heavy and leaden, and he would be grateful when he could finally lie down and rest.

The proprietor unlocked and opened the door. He stepped aside for Jesse to look, and what Jesse saw made his eyes widen: a large, rounded steel tub filled with water, steam rising from it in thick whisps. Jesse walked in.

"Enjoy," the proprietor said. Jesse heard the door close behind him. He walked over to the tub, slipping out of his coat. His boots were a little stiff, but they came off with a tug. Everything else he stripped off much easier. Naked, he plunged one foot into the water and felt the cathartic burn across his skin. He stepped in with his other foot, then steadily lowered himself into the steaming water.

To Jesse, pain had never felt so good.

He barely noticed as a plump, dark-haired woman excused herself as she came in, apologizing for the intrusion. She picked up Jesse's clothes, promising to return them nice and clean, and then swiftly left again. Jesse slid back, letting the water rise right up to his shoulders. He'd rest his eyes just for a minute, he thought, and then he'd get to scrubbing.

He wasn't sure how long it had been but when Jesse did finally open his eyes, the water was warm, and his clothes had returned in much better condition. He unraveled his bandage and washed. He then retired to bed in room number four and slept right through as soon as he lay back on the bed.

～

JONAH'S PULLING me by the arm again. I'm almost tripping because my little legs can't keep up with him. I do trip and fall in the mud. But Jonah just carries on up to the house, our little cabin in the woods. He opens the door, and it slams shut behind him.

I pick myself up and when I get to the door it opens all by itself.

It's not Jonah.

It's not Momma.

It's a man. His face is all blurry, but I know who he is. He's holding a piece of paper, all yellowed and creased.

"If anyone knows anything. It'll be him," he says and gives me the sheet of paper and tousles my hair and then closes the door—

∼

THE FOLLOWING DAY, Jesse sat at a table in the hotel, sipping a cup of coffee and watching the passersby outside the window. He reached into his coat pocket and pulled out a slip of paper, creased and yellowed with age. He knew what it said. And what it meant. But why had it been creeping up on him in his dreams?

Henry Pye sat down in the chair opposite Jesse, who, like himself, appeared a lot more presentable this morning. No more smudges on his face, cleaner clothes with the holes sewn or patched up. Irene had been busy.

"Good morning, kid," Jesse said. "How you feeling?"

"Clean. It feels *weird*."

Jesse laughed. "Don't get used to it. You'll get all dirty again anyway."

"I been thinking about what you said. About what I wanna be."

"And what's that?"

"I don't know."

"Can't have been thinking too hard, then." Jesse sipped his coffee.

"No." Henry's face screwed up like a piece of paper. Like the paper Jesse still had in his hand. Jesse pocketed it as the boy went on. "It's hard to explain . . . I know what I *don't* wanna be. I don't wanna be here. Running around looking for scraps to survive. I don't wanna be a guttersnipe."

"That's a good start. Knowing what you don't wanna be. Plenty of folks struggle with that question. The next part is much harder."

"What's the next part?"

"Figuring out what you *do* wanna be. You can't be or do what you want until you put away your past . . . and tie up any loose ends. I can't help you with that." Jesse sipped some more coffee while he considered his next words. "But I know of some folks who'll be able to look out for you and keep you safe while you figure it out for yourself."

"Can't I just come with you?"

Jesse laughed. "Trust me, kid, you don't want that." He felt bad as the kid chewed his bottom lip. "All I'm good at is finding trouble," Jesse said it as reassuringly as he could. He raised his coffee cup and glanced outside to see Irene. Her suitcase was on its side in the mud, and there was a man talking to her. No, more like talking *at* her. "Stay here, Henry." Jesse finished the last of his coffee as he got up from his chair, put the cup on the table, and left the hotel.

It looked bad from the inside, but outside it was much worse. Irene was a statue. Head bowed, shoulders hunched up and fists clenched by her sides. Her husband stood over her with a huge gut that strained the limits of his belt. He had a Stetson on, with wispy salt and pepper (mostly salt, Jesse noted) hair snaking out from under the brim behind his ears down to his shoulders. Jesse felt the sudden urge to buy a bowler or a slouch.

So, this was Clarence.

Clarence's cheeks were flushed, his eyes bulging with a rage that seemed reserved only for his wife, and his fat worm of a mustache danced as he spoke. He was berating her, sending foamy flecks of spittle all down his black neckerchief.

Jesse had seen enough.

He walked over, reached down and fished the case out of the mud and stood it back up on the deck of the hotel. "Sorry, Miss. This yours?"

Clarence's demeanor shifted in an instant. His back straightened and his shoulders relaxed. His gut jostled as he spun to face Jesse and shot him a grin full-to-bursting with charm. The kind of grin Jesse had seen on Eddie's face when they'd first met. "Why, yes, it is." His tone had changed, too. A lighter, more pleasant sound than the derisory barks aimed at his wife. "Thank you, sir. That is mighty kind of you." Clarence's voice sounded unsettling. Like a nice song played in the wrong key, something about it just felt uncomfortable.

"I was talkin' to the lady," Jesse said. He stood up to his full height, feeling a few vertebrae and a rib crackle. He clenched his teeth through the pain, suddenly hoping he wasn't going to have to come to blows with this man. "I see that she looks quite upset."

"Thanks for your concern, sir. She's just a little stirred up from the commotion with the train, y'see. Once I get her home, I'm sure she'll feel right as rain." Clarence followed it up with another grin. He turned to Irene and said, "Come on, darling. Let's get you home." He moved to take her by the arm and Jesse saw it. Easy to miss, but not to him. The tightening of her jaw and the clenching of her fists. Her knuckles would be white as salt under those gloves, he reckoned.

"Wasn't talkin' to you," Jesse said, raising a finger.

Clarence froze. His smile faltered for just a second. "'Scuse me?"

"I was talkin' to Miss Berg." Jesse put his hands on his hips, casually pushing back his coat to reveal the Colt nestled in its holster. "Not you."

Clarence's mouth fell open. He looked from Jesse to Irene. "Berg? *Berg*? You've been going by your maiden name, too? Irene, how could you?" Clarence turned back to Jesse, talking like she was cattle to be bartered. "She's not well, you see. Her mind gets clouded and hazy like it don't belong to her no more. This isn't the first time she's run away from me. With my money. That I earned to provide for her. For us. I keep her safe and—"

"Slap her around a bit when you feel it," Jesse said. That hit Clarence like the back of a hand. Several passers-by cast their judgments with looks of disdain. "She even did you the favor of waiting long enough for it to heal before running. Doesn't sound like somebody who ain't well in the head. Takes a good eye to spot that shiner you gave her." Jesse flashed him an Eddie Bradshaw shit-eating grin. "I got good eyes."

A nervous chuckle escaped Clarence's mouth. He looked a little redder now as he cleared his throat. "I'm not quite sure what you're getting at there, partner."

"Oh, I think we both are," Jesse said. "Like I said, I got good eyes. And I see through you like glass, Clarence." Jesse softened his words as he addressed Irene. "Miss Berg, could you get your husband's money out, please?"

Irene took two slow steps away from her husband, bent over her muddied case, and opened it up. She dug around in there for a moment. She stood up and moved beside Jesse, holding something wrapped in a handkerchief. Her head wasn't bowed anymore, her shoulders not quite as sunken. Jesse took the handkerchief from her gently and then tossed it to Clarence. Not expecting it, he scrambled trying to catch it, almost fumbling it into the mud.

"There's your money. She owes you nothin' now. You can go on your way." Jesse said.

"You think it's that easy? You think you can just pay me off with my own money? I'm not just gonna leave you here, sweetheart!" Clarence shifted forward, raising the cash.

"Take another step, Clarence," Jesse said flatly, "it'll be the last thing you do." The fat husband stopped, looking at his wife. "I guarantee it."

"You won't shoot me. You'll be hanged within the week if you do," Clarence said.

"I wouldn't count on it. Miss Berg here just helped save that train she was on. I'm fairly sure the marshals and the sheriff will believe her when she says it was self-defense."

"He came at you with a knife. I saw it," Henry said, head hanging out of the window of the hotel. Goddamn, if Jesse wasn't already a fan of that kid, he was now.

Clarence's Adam's apple bobbed in his throat.

"Go ahead. Take a step," Jesse said.

"Yeah, Clarence!" Henry yelled from the window. "Go on, get!"

Clarence stared at his wife in a way that she had probably seen a thousand times before. Beneath the façade of his smile, teeth gritted and eyes bulged in their sockets. Clarence's mask strained to contain the tempest beneath. Jesse could see that rage that boiled in his eyes: a master without his whip unable to exert control. Irene stared right back at her husband, unblinking and unbroken. His hold over her was broken, and it was there for all to see.

The mask broke into that discomforting smile. "Okay. Very well. If that's what you want, my dear. When you're ready to come home, I'll be waiting," Clarence said. He looked over at Jesse, "She'll be back."

Jesse smiled and nodded.

Clarence turned away and plodded through the mud.

Irene was now shivering. The tension quite literally shook its way out of her. Jesse wrapped himself around her and felt her shudder against his body, each one jabbing fresh pain into his ribs. He took each stab with a smile. He felt her sobs come next, deep, raw, and ugly. And so very necessary.

Jesse was just glad to be of assistance.

∼

BACK INSIDE THE HOTEL, Irene was much calmer as she clasped a cup in both hands. Henry chewed a piece of bacon, the plate in front of him loaded with strips of it.

"Thank you, Jesse," Irene said from above her cup.

"I barely did anything. You're the one who got yourself out of it."

"But you were there with me. I don't think I could have if you weren't."

"I *really* wanted to shoot him, though," Jesse said. Irene giggled over her cup. "Just shoot that stupid mustache right off his face, you know?" That got Henry laughing, too.

"I have no idea what I'm going to do now. I have a suitcase full of clothes and three dollars to my name. And yet, it scares me less than being in the same room as that man."

"Well," Jesse began. "I have an idea that might suit the both of you—"

Sarah Grahame burst through the door and into the dining room. "Clayton. Up you get."

"You found them?"

"Hell, yes, we did. Now come on!"

Jesse left the table for a second time that morning. "Hold that thought!" He said and ran out of the hotel after Sarah.

13

X MARKS THE SPOT

They arrived in Shellow after a few hours' ride. The afternoon sun was baking up the ground again, sending up heat lines in the distance as they rode.

Sitting on the plains a few miles west of Rathdrum, Shellow was by all means shallow. It was modest and quiet, the kind of place a man would rest himself and his horse to break up a long ride. It had a stable with a wonky wooden roof, and a saloon that didn't even have a name above its door. Its windows were mostly boarded up, and the ones that weren't were either cracked or broken in. Opposite that was what they'd come for: a two-story hotel, complete with a balcony. That was it, nothing else but the road that stretched for miles either side of it. Less of a town and more of a rest stop.

Jesse, LeFleur, Sarah, and Ben Marsden left their horses at the back of the saloon. The whole ride up, Marsden kept looking over at Jesse, shooting him a grimace on his boyish face like Jesse was something nasty he'd stepped in. Marsden was young, and probably figured Jesse was a threat. The kid must have been boiling underneath his denim jacket, jeans, and riding gloves.

"So, what're we doin', boss?" Marsden asked LeFleur, eager as he was. Jesse wondered how long he'd been part of LeFleur's outfit. It couldn't have been long, given the unimpressed raised eyebrow Marsden got as an answer. He looked down and then away, catching sight of Jesse. Marsden quickly covered his embarrassment with anger. "What's your problem?"

"Nothing," Jesse said, grateful for the opportunity to put the kid in his place. "Just wondering how long the Marshal Service has been recruiting children."

Sarah laughed, and even LeFleur let slip a faint smile.

Marsden, however, was less impressed. "I ain't a kid."

"You sure ain't a lawman, either."

"Oh, yeah? How would you know?"

"I can just tell." Jesse looked over at Sarah. "This the kind of fool you're runnin' with these days?"

"Hey, you're the one who got tired of it, not me," Sarah said.

"Hey! I'm talkin' to you, drifter!" Marsden's whiny voice was starting to irritate Jesse.

"You killed a man yet, Marsden?"

Marsden faltered. "Well, no . . . not yet. But we ain't needed to."

"You will soon enough, and then we'll see how much of a marshal you are. I just hope that day ain't today." Jesse looked to LeFleur. "He ain't coming along, is he?"

LeFleur grunted and stuck his thumbs in his belt. "He is. He might be greener'n grass but he's a hell of a shot with that iron. Even better with a repeater. He'll stick with me. I want you and Grahame to take point. Flush out these train robbers o' yours, and we'll sweep 'em up along with the dust. We'll get these bastards, dead or alive." LeFleur raised a bushy white eyebrow at Jesse. "I assume you can identify them?"

Jesse nodded.

"Then there's no time like the present."

∽

JESSE AND SARAH hugged the wall of the saloon. The tavern cast a long shadow across the road, the sun well on its way down again.

Time felt awful fast just lately, Jesse thought. He eased his head out to get a view of the hotel across the road.

A couple was dining in the restaurant, but not the couple that they were after. A man in a soiled apron stood on the decking out front sweeping the planks. Upstairs, Jesse couldn't see much of anything. One room on the end had its curtains closed, quite the odd fish at this hour. Maybe that was something.

He nodded at Sarah and the two of them crossed the road at a brisk pace. As they walked, Jesse looked back at the nameless saloon. Inside the entrance, he saw Ephraim smoking a cigarette. No sign of Marsden, which probably meant he was tucked away somewhere watching all this through an eyeglass on top of a Springfield.

Sarah waved her star at the man with the broom, and he stopped immediately.

"We're looking for a man and a woman," Sarah said, using what Jesse used to call her bounty hunter voice. A touch gruffer and an octave deeper, mostly for show. She had to put up with a lot of crap on account of her gender, and she'd found that this cut through a lot of it relatively quickly. Jesse preferred it to when she'd just hit people. "Who've you got stayin' here today?"

"Uh, just the two rooms currently," the man said. His spectacles sat wonky across his nose. He looked grubby, like he was coated in the grime and dust that blew down the road. "Two couples. One is dining currently—"

"Not the ones we're lookin' for," Jesse said. "What about the other couple?"

"Upstairs. Room Two."

"They still in there?" Sarah asked.

"Since they checked in yesterday. In fact, I ain't seen the two of them today at all."

"And what do they look like?"

"He was blond. Thick hair all swept back like young folks like him do now. Her. Well, she was bee-yewtiful. Hair redder than fire."

Sarah looked to Jesse who gave her a nod. "Sounds like them."

She turned back to the man. "Gonna need a key to room two unless you wanna be buying a new door."

The man dropped his broom and fished out a ring of keys. They jangled as his shaking hands searched for one in particular. After a few seconds and mumbled curses, he produced a key. Sarah took it and told him to find cover. And to tell the same thing to the other couple too. She pulled her Smith and Wesson and gestured with it for Jesse to follow. He pulled out his Colt and tailed her into the hotel and down the hall.

They took the L-shaped stairs as quietly as they could. They were careful not to stress the creaking boards too much as they went up, but the odd grunt crackle from the wood was unavoidable. At the top of the stairs, Sarah took point, crossing the landing with Jesse in tow until she reached the door with a brass '2' that hung at a slight angle.

They waited in silence for a moment, listening. No voices. No movement. But there was definitely *something* going on in there. A faint rustling sound and a staccato muffled grunt. Somebody in there was either in great discomfort or having themselves a good time. Jesse and Sarah exchanged a glance. She slipped the key into the lock, ready.

She knocked on the door.

The noises stopped.

She knocked again. "United States Marshal Service. Open up."

Inside, the shuffling sound returned at a much quicker pace, the muffled grunting a lot more panicked now.

She banged on the door. "I say again, this is the United States Marshal Service. You have to the count of three to open up this door or else we will open it by force." She projected her bounty hunter voice loud enough to carry through that door.

Jesse couldn't help but smile. "Just like old times, right, Sarah?"

She smiled back. "Be ready on that door." Then, louder, "*One.*"

More flustered shuffling and grunting from the other side of the door. "*Two.*"

The moment Sarah said *three*, Jesse twisted the key and then the handle. Keeping low, he pushed the door open. Colt raised, he stepped inside the room. It wasn't particularly big. The curtains were closed, but there was enough sunlight spilling in through the gaps to see what was what. A dresser in one corner was party to a belt holster, complete with dual pistols. On the chair next to it rested a very familiar-looking pecan gambler, while scuffed cavalry boots, a shirt, and a khaki jacket were all strewn across the grimy floorboards.

It was the bed that drew Jesse's attention, though. So much so that he stopped in his tracks. He lowered his gun as well as his jaw, not quite sure he was seeing what he was seeing. Covered in sweat and with terror in his eyes, Eddie Bradshaw was tied to the bed, each limb secured to a post, stretching him out like a cross.

X marks the spot, I guess.

～

"BARE-ASS NAKED?" Ephraim LeFleur shouted from down below outside the saloon.

"Yes, sir," Sarah said, half propped out the window. "He ain't leavin' nothin' to the imagination."

"Any sign of the girl?"

Sarah shook her head.

LeFleur blew smoke from his nostrils. "Get him dressed and get him down. I wanna beat the sun to Rathdrum."

Inside, Jesse had spared Eddie's blushes by repositioning the man's gambler. He also removed the handkerchief that had been stuffed in his mouth. When he did, he saw it wasn't fresh. Wiping his hands, Jesse sat down on the edge of the bed, being sure to check it was clean first.

"Where is she, Eddie?"

"I don't know."

"Come on now, don't be like that."

"I *don't*. My friend, *look* at me. This is not how I imagined things would play out when she suggested it last night. If I knew where she was, I'd be singing it to you the moment you took that damn-filthy handkerchief outta my mouth. She played me!"

"I told you I'd find you, Eddie," Jesse said. He was tempted to grin but thought he'd be the bigger man. "I just didn't think it would turn out quite the way it has. I reckon you didn't either."

"Fancied it to be a big duel between us, huh?" Eddie said. He glanced over at his guns on the dresser. "You know, it could still go down like that."

"No, it won't. As much as I'd like to put a bullet right through you for what you did on that train, you're gonna face the law instead. You don't deserve frontier justice. My guess is you'll escape the noose. I hear Yuma's quite nice this time of year."

"Come on now, Jesse. Surely there's something we can work out with your marshal friend here?" Eddie said. It was interesting to see how a man's demeanor changed along with his prospects. Gone was the boyish charm and the confident tone. His voice was crackly now, desperate and frantic. His eyes were wide and begging. That was the thing about a man well overdue a fall: when they finally do drop, they hit the ground hard enough to break.

"Even if there was, you ain't got the paper to make it. Roxie's halfway to anywhere with it all. Save your begging, Eddie. It's over." Jesse kept his voice level, as much as he wanted to rub it in, this was official marshal business. He did have one thing on his mind, though. "Just out of curiosity, how much money was in that safe?"

"Honestly? I don't know," Eddie said glumly. "Stopped counting at twenty thousand."

Jesse let out a long whistle. *Twenty thousand dollars. At least.* It did make him wonder if he'd have been tempted had the cash just been sitting there. He and Winona would be quite well off with that kind of money.

Money dipped in blood, Jesse reminded himself.

"Cut him loose," Sarah said, then to Eddie, "Get dressed and get downstairs. Do anything funny and I'll clip you in the leg. Understand?"

Eddie nodded.

Jesse cut Eddie free of his restraints. Then the two of them left him in the room to change, Jesse grabbing his gun belt on the way out. They got about halfway down the creaking stairs before they broke out into a fit of laughter.

∽

IN THE SHERIFF'S office in Rathdrum, Jesse watched Eddie Bradshaw sit down on the bench behind the black iron bars of the holding cell. It gave him a sense of satisfaction to see him there. A stark contrast from the well-groomed, sharp-looking killer he'd been on the train, now he was untucked, disheveled, marred with dust in his hair and pores. But it was the solemn look on his face. That look of defeat in his eyes. This felt better than putting a bullet in him, he realized. Knowing that every one of his days going forward would be just like this. Watching the world pass him by from behind bars.

Jesse approached the bars. Eddie raised his head and the two of them eyeballed one another.

"You enjoy your stay," Jesse said. "This is about the best you'll have it from here on in. Make the most of it."

"I will get outta here, Jesse. Mark my words." Eddie's eyes had a fervor to them as he spoke. "I promise you I will be free again one day. And you and I, we'll finish what we started today."

Jesse folded his arms. "Is that so?"

Eddie nodded furiously. "Absolutely. I promise you. I'll get out."

"Sure you will, Eddie."

"And then maybe I'll go pay a visit to your girl . . . Winona, was it?" Eddie flashed Jesse a shit-eating grin. Jesse gritted his teeth. He wanted to rip the bars apart to get to him in that moment. But that would be exactly what Eddie wanted: a reaction.

"Clayton." Sarah's voice came from out front.

"Goodbye, Eddie," Jesse said and then turned away from the bars.

14

HERE, CALIFORNIA, OR THE GODDAMN MOON

Outside, LeFleur and Marsden were with the sheriff. Sarah was leaning against the wall beside the door, watching the street and waiting with an envelope. When Jesse stepped out, she handed it to him.

"What's this?" Jesse said, opening it up. Inside was money. At least a hundred dollars, at a glance.

"Call it payment for services rendered. Between whatever you did on the train to keep folks alive and helping to bring in most of the robbers, LeFleur talked the locals into a bounty fee. I'd say you've earned it."

Jesse shrugged. "Four out of five ain't bad, I guess." He dipped his hand into his pocket, expecting to find the rest of his money. Instead, he felt the crinkle of paper. He pulled out the creased, stained, folded note. He considered it a moment.

"What's that?" Sarah asked.

"A loose end," Jesse said. He pocketed it again and fished around the rest of his pockets until he found his money. Once he did, he tucked the bills into the envelope with the bounty money. "Thank you, Sarah."

"So, how 'bout it? You join up, me and you back together again, like old times?"

"I think I've had enough excitement for one day."

"Oh, come on, Jesse." She playfully elbowed him in his bad ribs. He tried his best to act like they weren't on fire. "I promise I won't try and kiss you if that's what you're worried about."

Jesse laughed, mainly to cover the pain. "Looks to me like you've got plenty of help, with LeFleur and your young gun, Marsden. Suits you being all lawed up and official."

"Pays well, and it's nice to have the money regular rather than waiting contract to contract. Besides, LeFleur is about ready to throw up the sponge. He puts it out there he's still a quick-wristed son of a bitch, but I see him some mornings when his joints creak and it takes him twenty minutes to piss. And Marsden . . ." Sarah frowned. The kind of frown one would wear when regarding a disappointing sibling. "He means well, but he's too eager to please."

"That'll change once he gets his first kill," Jesse said. "Just give him time. We were like him once."

"*You* maybe."

Jesse laughed again.

LeFleur shook the sheriff's hand, gave him a swift nod, and then walked over to Jesse and Sarah. "The sheriff will keep hold of Bradshaw until it's decided where he's gonna be tried. There ain't gonna be any break-out attempts, d'you think, Clayton?"

Jesse shook his head. "His friends are dead, and I really doubt his woman's gonna rush back to rescue him. She's got enough trouble avoiding paper cuts."

LeFleur chuckled. "Funny as well as resourceful. You know, Clayton, you'd make quite the marshal."

"I bet I would."

"Not something you're interested in?"

"Afraid not, Ephraim. I got plans for something else."

"All right. I respect that." LeFleur extended a liver-spotted hand, little more than skin hanging on bones. "Thank you for the help. I hope you find the compensation satisfactory."

"Very satisfactory," Jesse said and clasped it, careful not to squeeze too tight. A decision he regretted when he felt the crush of LeFleur's grip. Jesse had the feeling Sarah may be wrong about him retiring fairly soon. He struck Jesse as the kind of man who would need to be stopped, instead of calling an end to things himself. "Take care, now."

"You, too. Hopefully, we'll work together again soon," LeFleur said. He gave Sarah a nod and then walked away toward his horse.

"These plans you have, they involve a woman?" Sarah said.

"How'd you guess that?"

"Oh, come on, all those bounties we got together, not once have you ever had anything in mind other than where you were getting your next meal. Now all of a sudden, you've got a plan? Only thing that changes a man like that is a woman."

She had a point. As blunt as she was, Sarah always had a knack for hitting a nail squarely on the head. It was part of what made her such a damn good bounty hunter, and now a U.S. Marshal. She was a damned good shot too, but not quite as good as Jesse, in his opinion, at least.

"I have a place to go, I just . . . I'm not sure if there's somethin' I should do first."

"Is it that loose end in your pocket?"

"Jesus, Sarah, get out of my head." At times that bluntness was downright unnerving.

"Ask yourself this: are you gonna be able to tear up that piece of paper and go to your woman without it ever crossing your mind again? 'Cus if you can't do that, you'll never be able to rest easy with that lady no matter where it is you go. Here, California, or the goddamn moon. It'll always be there at the back of your mind, gnawing at you like a rat in your crawl space."

Jesse nodded. "Can't really argue with you there."

"You used to. Over anything and everything. You really have changed, Jesse."

"A good woman'll do that to a man. Guess that says a lot about you," Jesse said with a sly grin.

She called him a son of a bitch and pulled him in for a hug he knew he wasn't getting away from. She wasn't big, but she was strong. And truth be told, he'd missed her a lot. As usual, she'd been there at the right time to say just what he needed to hear. It would have been nice to have had her backing him up on the train, though, he supposed.

She let him go and started to walk away. "You ever get to Spokane and need any money, check the sheriff's office there. There's a few good bounties up there paying pretty well. Easy money for you, Jesse."

"I'll keep it in mind. Take care of yourself, Sarah."

"See you around, Jesse Clayton."

JESSE SAT at the table with Irene and Henry again. "Now, I get that this is a big ask, Irene, and I'm not asking you to be Henry's mother, but I think that having you there together would make it easier for both of you. I can't make either of you go, but I can guarantee that if you do, you'll be looked after by people that I trust, while you figure out your way in the world."

Jesse reached into his coat pocket and pulled out his envelope. He took out a few bills for himself and then placed it down on the table and slid it across. The money was supposed to be for him and Winona and their big fresh start, but somehow, he thought she wouldn't mind it going to these two.

"What is that?" Irene asked. Suspicion hung in her eyes.

"That's for the both of you. To help get you started down there. Fortune ain't much right now, but it will be. Like the two of you, it's in the midst of its own fresh start."

"Where exactly is it?" Irene asked.

"A few miles from here. And the ranch you'll be staying at is not far beyond that. Bill's an old grump, but he's a good man who could use some company, I reckon. As for what you can do? Bill could always use a ranch hand, or you speak to my friend Frank in town, he'll be able to help you get started. Just don't let him talk you into whorin'."

Irene snapped back, her mouth wide with shock. "Mr. Clayton, I am *not* that kind of woman."

"You be sure to tell Frank that. He's a persuasive man." Jesse turned to Henry. "Kid, I'm not sure what you wanna do, but I can tell you now, if you're as set on being somethin' different as you were yesterday, Fortune's your best chance at making it happen."

Henry nodded. "I'll go."

Jesse smiled. "Miss Berg?"

"I will go with the boy," Irene said. "Is there a general store in this *Fortune*?"

Jesse nodded.

"I've always wanted to run my own store. Maybe I'll inquire there."

"You do that."

With perfect timing, Tobias Wilkerson entered the restaurant, hat in hand. He introduced himself to Henry and Irene before Jesse explained that he'd be their ride into Fortune. "Tobias is a good man, just don't buy his tonic. He'll get you into town, introduce you to Bill and Frank and help you get settled in." Jesse slipped a dollar to Tobias under the guise of a handshake. "Isn't that right, Tobias?"

"Absolutely. Are we ready to depart now? If we do, we'll make it with plenty of time before sundown." They all rose from the table and said their goodbyes. Henry wrapped himself tightly around Jesse, and he was unsure of what to do. He settled with patting Henry on the back, then kneeling in front of him.

A tear ran down the kid's left cheek. "I'm gonna miss you, Jesse."

"I'm gonna miss you too, kid. But I'll come visit sometime. I promise. And when I do, you be ready to impress me, okay?"

Henry nodded ardently, biting back his bottom lip and a bout of sobs.

Jesse extended his hand. "Goodbye, Henry Pye." The kid grabbed his hand and squeezed it as hard as he could. Jesse pretended to cry out in pain. "Quite the grip there, kid." Underneath the puffy eyes and tears, Jesse Clayton saw a smile.

"Goodbye, Jesse Clayton," Henry said.

Irene gave Jesse a departing hug and said her goodbyes too. Then, Tobias, Irene, and Henry left the hotel, and Jesse watched through the window as they walked down the street. Henry turned and gave one last wave, and Jesse waved back.

～

JESSE STEPPED out of the Western Union, having sent another message to Winona informing her of a further delay and where he was headed. He would send word in more detail in a letter that would reach her at her address in San Francisco.

He walked through Rathdrum, minding his way through the crowd. Tipping his hat and greeting folks, minding wagons and horses, all the while thinking about what he was about to do. He knew what he wanted. He wanted to be with Winona Squires in San Francisco. But like he'd told Henry and Sarah had told him, he couldn't have any loose ends lingering to be pulled at again and again. His past was behind him.

It needed to stay that way.

Jesse had done many things in an effort to atone. Maybe now he could start to take something for himself. But first, he had to know. To answer the question that for many years had long burned at the back of his mind.

He pulled out the piece of paper in his pocket and opened it up, just to make sure it still said what it had always said, written in that same spider scrawl handwriting:

Lonnie Compton
Bleaker's Creek
Missoula, Montana

He closed it up again and put it back. It was decided: he'd put his past to bed and then get on with his future. A short trip to Montana for some closure and then he could get on with his life. A life with a beautiful woman he could call his . . . what exactly? Still not sure about that label, he'd have to do something about that the next time he saw her.

Jesse approached the ticket booth. The same plump woman from yesterday pushed up her glasses as she bluntly asked him, in that terribly nasal voice, where he was headed.

"Missoula, please," Jesse said. He thought for a moment, then added, "First-class." He quite enjoyed the notion of having the luxury of a table; those benches had looked a lot more comfortable, too.

"Okay, no problem. Now, is that a one-way ticket, sir?"

"Oh, hell," Jesse said. "I hope not."

Printed in Great Britain
by Amazon